DAYS OF TORTURE

DAYS OF TORTURE

WRITTEN BY *Cynthia Cluxton*

Order this book online at www.trafford.com
or email orders@trafford.com

Most Trafford titles are also available at major online book retailers.

The following story is fiction. None of the names or events are real.

Printed in the United States of America.

ISBN: 978-1-4269-3741-5 (soft)
ISBN: 978-1-4269-3742-2 (ebook)

 www.trafford.com

North America & international
toll-free: 1 888 232 4444 (USA & Canada)
phone: 250 383 6864 ✦ fax: 812 355 4082

DEDICATION

This story is dedicated to my family. Thanks for their support and for putting up with me while writing this book. Thanks to my best friend W. A. T. for listening to me and for her support and encouragement. Thanks for the encouragement and motivation from everyone. Thanks to my grandkids! I didn't spend the time I normally would have with them due to the writing of this work. I am truly sorry.

Special thanks to my husband for not getting aggravated and for listening to me describe and tell him about this writing (story)!

I am most thankful to God for giving me the writing ability, strength and courage to do this work. I give God the praise and love for anything anyone may get from this story. It is intended to show that no matter what we may go through in life, there is a higher power than ourselves.

Things may not always go the way we want them to go or when we want them to, but if we trust in God and believe in him, he will see us through everything. Sometimes we may question God's reasons but he has a plan!!!

With all my love, Cynthia Cluxton

Contents

CHAPTER 1

IN THE BEGINNING
MY CHILDHOOD MEMORIES

I remember when I was eight years old. It was nearing Christmas time. While in my bedroom of our home in Michelle Tennessee, I was always daydreaming. I was thinking about the presents I would be opening on Christmas morning.

It was back in the time when most kids would get one toy for Christmas. Usually one would get a yo-yo or a paddle ball, where the ball was attached to a rubber band. Maybe some jacks and ball, or a bag of marbles.

If you were a girl and you were extra good, you might get a baby doll or baton. If you were a boy and extra good, you might get a gun and caps or maybe a push around toy car.

On this particular Christmas, I knew I had been good and I could hardly wait for Christmas morning so that I could open my presents! Yeah, I had two presents! I saw them under the Christmas tree. I had been snooping under the Christmas tree and had read the name on the handmade tags that were taped to the presents. It clearly read "Sandra Tucker"!!

As I was daydreaming, I knew from the size of my presents that there was something bigger than a yo-yo inside them! I knew there weren't jacks inside either. I couldn't figure what was inside them. My imagination was running wild. Finally, with no clue as to what might be inside, I decided to give up guessing and wait until Christmas.

Anxiously waiting for what seemed like forever, finally Christmas morning had arrived. I awoke from sleep way before daylight.

I jumped out of bed and ran down the stairs to the living room. The room was dark except for the light glowing from the fireplace and the colored lights that were hung on the Christmas tree.

I heard music. Momma had forgotten to turn off the radio when she went to bed. I could hear Christmas music playing softly from it! It was someone singing we wish you a merry Christmas.

I guess momma had heard me rambling around down stairs. It wasn't but just a minute or two that I heard her coming down the stairs.

I was jumping up and down as I said to momma, can I open my presents!

Momma, with her great big smile, said, first we need to wait for your great granny Tucker. She'd want to watch you open them.

The whole time I was waiting momma was shushing me to be quiet so I wouldn't wake great granny Tucker.

Great granny Tucker was my daddy's grandmother. While trying not to wake great granny Tucker, I was waiting very patiently, at least I thought I was!

Then, I heard her! She had finally gotten out of bed! I could hear her walking stick as it would make noise against the wood floor as she made her way to the living room!

I was excited! Here we were, Momma, great granny Tucker and I together for Christmas. I watched as momma lit some candles that set upon the mantel. It gave the room a glow and warmth like nothing I'd ever felt!

As I took my place on the floor in front of the Christmas tree, momma bent over and reached for the presents. She handed each of us our presents.

I tore into the paper and unwrapped the first present. It was a baton. I grabbed it up and began to march around and twirl it as if I were in a marching band. Momma and great granny Tucker were laughing with joy!

Then each of them opened a gift. I had colored them a picture from an old coloring book I had. I hoped they would like them! From the hugs and kisses I received, I knew they did!

Momma had given great granny Tucker a brand new apron. She had made it from scrap material she had stored away for some time.

Great granny Tucker gave momma her gift. It was a box of oatmeal cookies. She had made them from scratch from an old family recipe that had been passed down over the years. Everybody had gotten the perfect gift.

Then momma said, Sandra, don't forget that you have another present. I had gotten so caught up in watching as momma and great granny Tucker opened their gifts, I had forgot about my other one!

I grabbed up the present and tore the paper from the box. The box was taped shut. I tugged at the tape and finally it broke. I opened the box and inside was the most beautiful gift in the whole world! My eyes lit up!

I had gotten my very first baby doll for Christmas! I knew I had been a good girl! The doll was dressed in yellow and white. Her shoes were white as well. Her hair was chestnut color and tiny yellow bows were attached on both sides. She had the bluest eyes and dark eyelashes. She was beautiful!

I ran into momma's arms and hugged her and thanked her and told her I loved her! Great granny Tucker too!

Momma told me that Santa Claus had brought it! I didn't dare tell momma that I knew there wasn't a Santa! I didn't want to spoil her Christmas!

My momma had always looked forward to seeing the smile on my face at Christmas time. What momma didn't realize is the smile was of appreciation because I knew how hard she worked to be able to get me anything. I knew where my Christmas gifts came from!

Then sadness came over me! I looked up at momma and said to her, I wish daddy could be here. I told her I missed him so much. I watched as a tear then rolled down momma's face. Momma missed him too.

Momma had to raise me by herself with the help of great granny Tucker. My daddy died when I was five years old. He had worked in the coal mines.

The only thing I remember is daddy didn't come home one day. I remember momma saying that the mines had caved in on him and he wasn't able to get out. He'd left momma all alone to take care of great granny Tucker and me.

Christmas had come and gone. The doll I had gotten for Christmas was the greatest thing to me. The baton was a fun thing to play with, but my doll, I loved the best!

I cared for her just as if she was human. Momma had told me if I took good care of her, that when my next birthday came around, I could get another doll.

Sure enough, when my 9th birthday came, I had gotten another doll. She was just as precious as the first one. I guess I must have taken pretty good care of the first one! I know I had always made sure that she was put away when I finished playing with her and I had always made sure that her hair was neatly kept and she was always dressed properly and kept clean.

The baby dolls were my whole life, except for momma and great granny Tucker. I would fix my dolls hair and pretend to put makeup on them. They had to be just right. I would stay in my room seems like for hours playing beauty shop. I would run down stairs to show off how pretty I had made my dolls. I was so proud! Momma would just rave about how nice they looked.

As a child, to be nine years old, momma would always say that I was very smart for my age. I would tell momma and great granny Tucker that I wanted to be a beautician when I grew up! I'd been saying that for nearly two years. Momma even said to me that most kids my age wouldn't ever think about what they wanted to become.

I remember a time before I had ever gotten a baby doll. I guess I was about six years old. I think this is when I had made a choice of what profession I wanted to get into.

I had taken momma's mop from the broom closet and turned it upside down. I would pretend that the mop was a doll. I experienced doing a hair cut to the mop. The mop head was my model and I had cut the cotton strands to what I thought was a perfect haircut!

It wasn't until I had completely destroyed momma's mop that I realized that momma was gonna tan my hide when she found out what I had done! I actually thought I could put the mop back into the broom closet and momma wouldn't notice!

The next morning, after thinking I'd hid my mistake, and momma had served breakfast, she sent me up stairs to clean my room and she began her chores.

As I was up stairs making my bed, I heard momma holler my name. Sandra Tucker! I knew from the tone of her voice and the fact that she added Tucker to my name that she'd found the mop. I don't think I was able to set down for a few days after that day!

I sometimes wondered if maybe that's why momma had gotten me that first doll! I guess it was cheaper to buy a doll that I'd take care of, instead of having to replace mops all the time! I learned my lesson and never messed with another mop except for when I had to clean the floor with one!

I practiced my profession on other things too! I remember the times that I took in every stay animal that came in our yard.

I remember one huge yellow cat! I knew that someone had dropped it off. It was very healthy and clean. It was a long haired cat. I remember momma giving me an old brush and comb just so I could make the cats fur pretty! The cat seemed to like being brushed and combed. One day it just disappeared! Momma told me the cat was an old tom cat. I later learned that a tom cat was a male. He was in search for a mate.

I had taken in many dogs during my childhood. As with the cat, I groomed the dogs too. I once put hair bows in one of the pup's hair.

I once even took in a toady frog! I thought it was going to drown in the pouring rain. I can remember sneaking it up to my room and putting it in an old shoe box.

It wasn't that I thought I could groom the toad, but that I had a tenderness in my heart for all creatures.

When momma found out that I had taken in a frog, I thought she was going to have a stroke. She had come into my room one morning and heard a croaking sound. She asks me what the noise was that she had heard. I tried to let on like it wasn't anything, but after she did a search under my bed, she found the little toad.

When she pulled the box out from under the bed and opened it up, she quickly put it down and began to holler! She said to me "Sandra Tucker, what are you doing with a toad"?

I knew from momma's reaction that she didn't like the toady frog! She just shook all over as she made me take the toad outside and set it free! Momma didn't get very upset about me taking in the toad. She just told me not to bring another one in the house.

Along with the cat, the dogs and the toad; I had taken in a bird, a rabbit and a baby snake. The snake was the straw that broke the camels back so to speak!

Momma knew that I cared for every living thing, so it was when I brought the baby snake into the house that she set me down and tried to explain to me that I couldn't take in every thing that I thought needed my help!

I knew momma was right, but I was just a softy when it came to something or someone I thought needed my help.

Another of my many childhood memories that I recall is when one morning I had awakened just as the sun was coming up over the mountain.

I could smell bacon frying from the kitchen down stairs. I knew momma would be calling me to come down and eat.

I got out of bed and got my baby dolls. I was excited! Momma had given me some old nail polish and an old tube of her lipstick that was just about empty. I had never had real makeup before so this was going to be a special day.

To add to my excitement, momma had also taken some old scrap material and made a couple of new outfits for my dolls.

I dressed each doll so carefully. I put lipstick on their lips and used some for rouge. I painted their nails. I had mixed some of the nail polishes together and had gotten a color mixture I thought was just right for eye shadow. I fixed each dolls hair. I put ribbons and bows of bright colors in their hair for a finishing touch. I made those dolls so pretty.

My dolls were ready to be shown off. I didn't wait for momma to call me down for breakfast. I took my dolls into my arms and ran down stairs to the kitchen.

Tugging on momma's apron, as she stood over the cook stove stirring gravy, I'd said, momma, just look at em! Aint they pretty! I said, see great granny Tucker!

Great granny Tucker was doing her best to help momma with breakfast. Even though she barely got around and was old, she refused to give up trying to do things.

Momma said "Yes they are pretty, Sandra Tucker". They are just beautiful! Great granny Tucker agreed!

Then momma said to me, now how do you suppose to get that nail polish off your dolls?

At the time of applying the polish, I hadn't thought about getting it off. Momma would help me with that task later and give me a lesson about make up!

Momma and great granny Tucker said I had a talent. I didn't even know what the word talent meant, but it sure did sound wonderful.

You can guess, from that day on, I was sure I wanted to be a beautician.

I happily set the table for breakfast as momma had told me to do while dreaming of my TALENT!

I recall when Great granny Tucker was nearly 80 years old! I was fixing to be ten years old in a couple of months. I remember the long ride to the hospital. Great granny Tucker was sick. She had taken pneumonia.

I could see the worry on momma's face. I watched momma pray many times while we were in the hospital room where great granny Tucker lay in the hospital bed.

Then I saw momma crying! Momma and I held great granny Tuckers hand as she passed quietly to go be with the Lord. I miss her so much. I miss her encouragement. She was like a second momma to me.

I can still remember great granny Tucker's hair. I remember stroking her hair with my hand while watching her pass. It was soft as silk and snowy white. It was so long that it touched the floor when she would stand up. She kept it in a bun most of the time.

I remember when I used to ask her to let me brush it. She rarely refused. She would take her hair down and hand me her brush. I would brush, braid, tease and even tangle her hair. She never complained.

Every time that I would brush her hair, I would start rattling about wanting to be a beautician. She would always smile and say, in her granny voice, child, you can be or do anything you set your head to do. Just work hard and always pray to the Lord to guide you.

I knew from great granny Tuckers words and hugs that she had always given me, that she loved me as much as I loved her! Even though she's gone now, there's a part of her that will always be with me.

Another time that I remember is when I was in the sixth grade at the elementary school. I had a best friend that would come to my house and spend the night. She and I had many things in common.

The best thing that we had in common was that we both loved to fix hair! I was eleven years old and she was twelve. I kind of looked up to her since she was older. Although we did other things like jumping rope and bike riding, we always found time for playing beauty shop!

She would do my hair and I would do hers! She taught me how to apply make-up correctly to ones face! At least at the time, I thought she knew what she was doing!

A few years passed by. Somewhere along the way, my friend had gotten interested in boys. I didn't see her anymore. I heard she had to marry. What a waste! She was a fifteen year old girl with such great potential but got herself pregnant and married and gave up on her dreams!

I promised myself that I wouldn't let my dreams of becoming a beautician only be a dream!

Looking back now, I know that there were better things that a person could dream of becoming, and I know that there were better paying careers out there, but I wouldn't trade what I do for anything!

I know I did some crazy things as a child. But I learned from the things I did. And my talent, I'm sure momma and great granny Tucker were just being kind and supportive back then, but their praises helped me to become what I am today. Nearly thirty years later, I was still doing hair and still a little crazy!

CHAPTER 2

IN SEARCH OF A MANICURE SPECIALIST

It was a cool but sunny spring morning in Brownsboro Tennessee. It was a flashy town where I owned my own beauty salon. Fancy Hair & Nails. Its location was nearly fifty miles from my home in Michelle Tennessee.

The weather was perfect for the annual Brownsboro Potato Cook off! The governor of Tennessee would be giving a speech and present an award for the best potato recipe.

It was going to be a busy morning for us at the salon. Our appointment books were overloaded! I looked around to see if all my employees were here. I had a total of seven workers and it was days like this that I felt that I needed a few more!

As I gazed around the salon, I saw Patricia was at her work station and she was making sure she had enough hair sprays and lotions for the day! She was one of my stylist and a massage therapist. She's a married mother of two.

I looked over at Meagan's station. She's one of my hair washers and make up artist. She is single and the young age of twenty three. She had a load of shampoo bottles in her arms and was filling her cabinet for the busy day!

Then I turned to see Carolyn. She does hair washes, styles and make up! She's twenty eight years old and she was engaged to be married.

Next I looked over to Pam. She was another hair washer and make up artist! Pam is a single nineteen year old. She has been working here for a year. She was an excellent worker. She came here straight out of high school! She knew her make up very well. She knew what worked together! She kind of reminded me of the best friend I had back in elementary school. She was ready for the day!

Then I saw Anita. A twenty six year old bomb shell beauty! She has a steady boyfriend. She was as beautiful on the inside as she was on the outside! She has this silky black hair and dark brown eyes and dark skin to match. She was a looker! She would turn heads of both men and women! She made women jealous! She was another one of my stylist and a massage therapist. She, like the rest were preparing for the day ahead!

Then there was Jamie Malone! She was my manicure specialist. She was sort of the back bone of the salon.

Jamie was the oldest of all of us. She was the only other married one of the bunch. She was at her work station getting ready for a hectic day. She was a large black woman and always happy! She seemed to be in a strange mood this particular morning.

She was a very religious lady. I saw that she was praying. She had her head bowed down and her hand raise toward the ceiling. She didn't appear to be her happy self this day!

I guessed that it was the adrenaline going on! All of us seemed to have a little anxiety today!

Finally there was Tammy Jackson. Tammy was a jewel to all of us! She helped everyone with whatever she could. She could do hair; make up; facials; manicures and everything in between!

Tammy was a twenty two year old ball of fire! She was a single mother. She had this flaming red hair to go along with her sometimes hot headed personality! She was a tiny petite size four but though she was small she had a big and loud bark!

Tammy had a good head on her shoulders too! Very smart! She would go places if she could ever control her anger!

After seeing that everyone had gotten everything ready, I unlocked the salon doors. It was 8:00am. We had clients outside the salon waiting to enter!

Seems everybody in Brownsboro Tennessee needed a hair cut, a perm, or their nails done. There were some customers that just wanted us to do their make-up.
The talk of the town or should I say the talk in the salon for the past two weeks had been that everybody was going to out do the other on grooming for the potato cook off festivities!

People were gossiping about who would have the best dress or shoes? Whose hair would stand out in the crowd?

The way the talk was, you'd think it was going to be a beauty contest instead of a potato cook off!

The event would begin at 11:00am today. It was now 8:15am. My first client of the day was none other than the governor's wife!

While I was doing the hair on the Tennessee Governor's wife, my manicure specialist, Jamie Malone came over to me. Jamie was waiting on her client's nails to dry.

Jamie always had a spiritual smile. Her mood I thought I'd saw before opening the salon had dissipated. You just knew that Jamie was a woman of the Lord. She had so much love in her heart.

Anyway, when Jamie came over to me, she said; Sandy, can I talk to you about something? She said in private if I didn't mind!

I told her; sure! I would give her a holler as quick as I finished with the Governor's wife's hair. I told her I'd have only a few minutes to spare and it would have to be a quick talk!

As busy as we were, I knew that this must be serious! For Jamie to come to me in between working with a client was not like her. Otherwise, I would have put her off until a lunch break or other time.

Jamie said it wouldn't take long. She then turned and walked back to her client she had been working on.

When I got finished with the Governors wife, I hollered over to Jamie and said I was ready to speak with her. Jamie had finished with her client. With only a few minutes to speak, we went into the conference room.

It was a private room in the back of the salon. It was kind of like a small kitchen area. It stored a coffee maker and a table and chairs. It was also used as a break room whenever one of us needed to rest between appointments. We wouldn't be using it for any rest today. Especially not before 11:00am.Everyone of us would be covered up with clients until then!

As we entered the room, I closed the door behind us. I poured us both a cup of coffee. We sat down at the table with a cup of coffee in hand.

I reached for my cigarettes that I had placed on the break room table. I took one out and lit it and took a couple of draws from it. After exhaling the smoke, I ask Jamie what, if anything was wrong?

She began talking. She said; you know I've been working in salons for nearly twenty years. I've been here working for you for five years. I'm getting old; she said!

Jamie was every bit of the ripe old age of 56! I laughed and said to her; you're not old! I felt like I knew where the conversation was leading. I took another draw from my cigarette. I said to her, what's this all about!

She said, well, my husband is going to retire in a few days. He and I have been talking. She went on to speak. I'm thinking about leaving the salon. You know, just retire with my husband!

I didn't know what to say!

Jamie kept talking. He and I want to travel. We want to do some things before we really do get to old! She said frankly, Sandy; as of today, I'm giving you my two weeks notice. She didn't say another word.

I was quiet for a moment. I wasn't shocked! A little surprised maybe! But I understood what Jamie had said.

This explained her mood! I felt her desire and need to move on and spend time with her husband. I told her how much I appreciated her work she had done for me at the salon. I told her she would be hard to replace, but wished her all the best.

Jamie had truly been a blessing for me. She had been like a mother to me. Especially since the time that I'd lost my mother due to a stroke four years ago.

Jamie had been working for me for about a year when my mother was buried. She had been my confidant when I needed one. She encouraged me when I would get down on myself. It was going to be sad not to have her here to talk to anymore.

I put out my cigarette in the ashtray. I didn't want Jamie to see my sadness so I said laughingly, well come on! Let's get back to work! We've got a busy day ahead of us! I want to get all I can out of you before you leave us!

We walked back into the salon area. Everyone turned to look at us. Even the clients that were being prettied up looked around.

I could read the expressions on my employee's faces. You would think that someone had died! They knew very well that what went on behind those closed doors in the conference room was mostly never good.

I'd had just about every one of them behind those doors at some time or another. Whether by my choice or theirs, it was almost always a depressing outcome.

I remember taking Tammy in that room quiet often! She being the hot head she is! Other than that; Tammy was indispensable. She just never could keep her mouth shut!

I remember when one of our clients had arrived late for an appointment with Tammy. Tammy made such a scene about it; we lost that client quicker than she came into the salon doors. I had to take Tammy in the conference room to explain to her that regardless of what we think or feel that sometimes we needed to hold our tongues!

Once I had an employee call me in the room to discuss her pregnancy. She'd gotten knocked up she said! She didn't want to keep the baby! She couldn't afford it, she said!

At the time I couldn't give her any more money than she was already making, but told her she shouldn't give up her child. She ended up leaving the salon. She gave the baby up for adoption. I don't know what happen to her after that.

Anyway, as everyone's eyes were on Jamie and myself, I said; girls I've got some news. I just blurted out "Jamie is getting a divorce"!

They all had a shocking look on their faces! A couple of them hollered WHAT! Even the clients in the salon that knew Jamie looked surprised.

Then I said, no I'm just kidding! But Jamie is going to be leaving the salon. She and her husband are retiring together! We'll have two more weeks with her before she'll be leaving.

Everyone looked somewhat relieved that it wasn't a divorce, but sadly told her they'd miss her. The clients' that knew Jamie was going to miss her too!

Finally after a couple of seconds of chatter, we all got back to work. I was happy for Jamie, but I worried about who I'd get to replace her.

She was the best manicure specialist around. She fit in with all of us here at the salon like a glove.

I worried myself crazy for the remainder of the day! And though business had slowed down by 11:00am, luckily, the day had passed by quickly. I didn't realize how quickly until someone had said let's get ready to go home. I hollered yeah, lets do! I was tired! I was glad it was time to close up the salon for the day! After doing so, I went and got into my car and drove toward home.

Soon after getting home and relaxing for awhile on the couch, I thought I should begin the search for a replacement. I went to my computer and logged in.

Things sure had changed over the years. I remember when there was no such thing as a computer and the internet was unheard of.

Back years ago, what seemed like ages, if you needed help, you got it by word of mouth or from a sign that was posted in a store window front.

I posted a classified ad over the net. Then I called the newspaper and put an ad in the paper in search for a manicure specialist.

After I finished putting out the ad, I got up and headed to the kitchen. I was hungry! I fixed myself a sandwich and salad for supper. I took my food to the living room.

I lived by myself so I ate many of my meals in front of the TV. I turned on the TV and listened to the news and weather. I finished my food, leaving my empty salad plate on the coffee table.

I laid back on the couch and felt myself dozing off. The night was passing by. I was so sleepy; I thought I'd just sleep on the couch.

Instead, I made myself get up. It was bed time. I went into my bedroom and pulled back the cover on my bed. I crawled under the covers and pulled them up to my neck. I was glad that I didn't stay on the couch. I could feel the warmness of the cover as it touched my body. I thought this is just what I needed!

For awhile I slept, but then I awoke with so many thoughts going through my mind. I tossed and turned the rest of the night.

I was such a worrier. I had two weeks to find a replacement manicurist, but you'd thought I only had a day or two! Before I knew it, morning had arrived.

The next day at the salon was a busy day. We were covered up as the day before. We barely had time for lunch.

Even though the potato cook off was over and the winners had been chosen, you'd thought it was still going on. I guessed people were trying to keep up their image.

As busy as we were, I did find time to post an ad in the salon front window for HELP WANTED!

As the days went by and it was getting closer to Jamie's last day we were planning a going away party for Jamie. It would be a small and simple get together at the salon during work hours. We would have chips and dip, peanuts, finger sandwiches, mints, and punch.

We all chipped in a little bit of money to buy Jamie a gift. We picked out a wicker basket that held lotions and such in it for her.

Jamie's last day at work had arrived! I still hadn't found a replacement for the manicure specialist I needed. Jamie was going to be missed. We all had said our goodbyes and wished Jamie happiness with her retiring. Jamie was gone. The farewell party went well!

In the meantime, I had gotten a tremendous response from all of the ads I'd put out for the replacement, but nobody was chalking up to what we needed here at the salon.

I'd given so many interviews and viewed so many E-mails; I thought I was going to be sick. I was having no luck. I couldn't believe it. Two weeks and then some had passed by and my manicure specialist was gone and still I hadn't found a replacement.

Tammy, now my right arm, was having to do the manicures until I could find someone to replace Jamie. She didn't like doing nails, especially toe nails, pedicures, she'd say! She was begging me to hurry and find someone!

I told her I was doing all I could. I told her to be patient. God would send someone, I said! He knew what I needed I told her!

I didn't tell Tammy this, but I was worried! I wasn't sure if God was even listening to my prayers for help! I was impatiently waiting and wondering what I was going to do.

Finally, a couple of days later I was checking my E-mails from home. After reading the resume of a girl named Amber Lynn Newby, I was impressed!

I immediately got on the phone and called her references. Each reference said she did beautiful manicures and pedicures. Each said she was an excellent worker.

I didn't wait till morning. I called Amber on the telephone right away. I told her who I was and thanked her for her interest in working within my salon.

I questioned and quizzed her about manicures and the salon in general. She seemed very confident. She sounded very smart!

I hired her right over the phone! Besides, after all the negative interviews I had given and had run out of time and Tammy was getting aggravated; I didn't have a better choice.

I ask Amber when she could start working. She said she could begin working the following Monday. That would be great, I said to her! I was happy! Amber would arrive in less than a week.

Ambers resume showed her address to be in Kentucky. She said she would be driving down. She didn't want to fly. She didn't like airplanes.

During our discussion, I told her to arrive by 8 am sharp! She thanked me. I then thanked her. It was set. I told her that I looked forward to seeing her on Monday and then said goodbye!

The next morning was Wednesday. I arrived at the salon. I told my employee's that I had hired a girl for the position. Everybody was thrilled for me. Tammy was tickled to death! Tammy said "when's she coming"?

I told Tammy and the others that the new help should arrive in less than a week. I said she should be here Monday morning!

The rest of the week seemed to drag by. Business had slowed down. The potato contest had been long over with. The town was quiet. There wouldn't be any other events happening for a long while. Only our regular clients were coming in to be beautified!

We passed the slow time off by discussing what we thought this new girl would be like and just having girl talk about all kinds of things. Also, we were taking in all the gossip that was being told by the clients that came into the salon!

Soon it was Saturday evening. We closed the salon and everyone had left for the weekend. Now all I had to do was to wait for Monday morning!

CHAPTER 3

THE ARRIVAL OF AMBER

The alarm clock went off at 6:00am. It was Monday morning. I was dreading this day more than any other day in a long while.

As I lay in bed, I grabbed my cigarettes and lit one. My mind began to wander as I puffed on the cigarette.

The new girl Amber Lynn Newby would be coming today. Even though I had spoke to her over the phone when I hired her and she sounded so confident, I was again wondering what she would be like. With all of us at the salon talking about her the last few days, I was having second thoughts.

As badly as I needed a manicure specialist, I wasn't looking forward to the drastic change at the salon today. Had I made the right choice? I was worrying myself for nothing, I thought!

Amber would be coming all the way from Kentucky! That was another state away! But that wasn't to far from Tennessee though. It wasn't like coming from California or even New York. My thoughts went wild!

I began to pray for Amber and that her road trip to here would be a safe one. Amber had said to me on the phone that she was used to traveling. I knew that Monday morning traffic was always terrible.

I wondered if maybe she had already arrived in Tennessee. Maybe she was staying at a motel somewhere. I wondered if she would even show up today. I rubbed my forehead to ease the tension I was feeling. I needed to stop worrying!

Maybe my morning shower would help! I put out my cigarette. I got out of bed and went into the bathroom. I removed my sleep clothing. I turned the shower on and stepped inside. The hot water felt good on my naked skin.

My mind was working over time. I still couldn't stop thinking about Amber and hoping that she would make it to Tennessee alright or even show up. I stayed in the shower until the water was getting cold. I turned off the water and stepped out to dry myself. I wrapped my towel around myself and went to my bedroom as I continued to worry.

I looked into my closet. I didn't know what I wanted to wear. I grabbed out a couple of outfits. One outfit was a pair of black pants and a baby blue top. The other was a black skirt that went with a pink flowery top. I tried each outfit on. Finally I had made up my mind. I chose the pants with the blue top. Soon I was ready for work.

I looked into my dresser mirror. I sure was ageing I thought. My clothes made me look fat! I was having second thoughts about what I had chosen to wear. It was too late to change. It really didn't matter, because when I arrive at work, I'd just cover up with one of those white work overcoats! Why was I worrying about that!

Then I once again had begun to wonder about the new girl Amber. Not that it mattered but would she be skinny or would she be fat? I wondered how she would dress. Was

Amber going to be as good as her former employers had said she was?

Lord, I was going to be late for work! I needed to stop worrying! I took another look in the mirror. I just sighed with disgust as I exited my bedroom!

I then went to the kitchen. I grabbed a quick pop tart and a glass of orange juice for breakfast. I quickly chugged it down. There was no time for my usual cup of coffee. I'd grab a cup at work, I thought!

Headed back to my bedroom, I gathered my work bag and purse. I fumbled through my purse for my car keys as I headed toward the living room to leave for work. As always they were all the way in the bottom of my purse. With keys in hand, I locked the front door to my house as I exited. I went to my car and headed out.

As I was driving toward work, again I wondered, prayed, that this new girl, Amber Lynn would fit in. I began to think about the client's that always came into the salon. Many of them were celebrities. Then there were all the locals. All of my clients were important. I hoped they would like Amber's work! I hoped they would like Amber! God, please let her do good I said to myself!

The drive to work seemed longer than normal. Finally, I pulled up in front of "FANCY HAIR & MANICURES" salon. I parked my car. As I sat in the driver seat of my car, I took a deep breath.

I looked through my windshield of my car and into the windows of the salon. I thought, as I do almost every day, I own this place! I worked hard to get it! I'd bought it 18 years ago.

I had done just like my great granny Tucker had always said to do. I had worked hard, in fast food chains and other odd jobs, when I was a teen and had saved every penny. I always prayed a lot! I put myself thru beauty school and here

I am. My dream. Today will be great. Just trust in God. He had always been there in my time of need.

I got out of my car. I walked to the salon doors and unlocked them. I took another deep breathe. I went inside.

Something seemed different about today! Not one of my employees had arrived yet. I was worrying that some of them might not make it in to work. Or maybe I wasn't as behind schedule as I had thought I was. My employee's were rarely late and rarely missed work! I put my hands up to my head to try to stop the worry!

I said to myself while shaking my head, Get it together Sandy! Finally I did! I had about ten minutes to get things ready to open by 8:00am. I put the salon money in the cash box and unlocked the doors to the salon. I then went and checked the setting on the air conditioner. It seemed hot in the salon. Maybe it was just me!

Soon the chimes on the salon door begin to chime. The employees were coming in for work. By 7:55am all of my employees were here and had gotten ready to start the day. All except for Amber Lynn Newby.

Again, I wondered if she would show up! Had she changed her mind! Had she had trouble getting here from Kentucky? If so, surely she would have called! Tammy was even questioning me about Amber's arrival! Then about two minutes before 8:00am, I heard the chimes on the entrance door again.

I looked around and saw this brown haired, green eyed, nearly six foot tall, kind of tomboy looking girl! Her hair was shoulder length and straight as a board! She didn't have any make up on her face. Fair skinned.

She was wearing boy cut blue jeans with a white t-shirt. She wasn't fat! She wasn't skinny! Not at all ugly. She was just kind of plain looking. If this was Amber, none of us had her pictured like this girl that stood before us looked!

One of my employees, Pam, greeted her and pointed her to my direction. The girl walked over to me and said with a shy and nervous kind of voice, Hello, I'm Amber Lynn Newby! I hope I'm not late.

She sounded different than she did on the phone. She didn't have that confident sound in her voice!

I said no you're not late, but I was beginning to worry. I'm glad you made it all right. I thought you might have changed your mind!

The next time she spoke wasn't as nervous sounding but still a little shy. She told me that the traffic was bad. She said that there had been an accident on the interstate that had the traffic backed up for miles.

She told me she had stayed in a motel room overnight. It was just a few miles from the salon. She said she never dreamed there would have been an accident and then she apologized for worrying me.

I think she was afraid that she wasn't going to get the position. I reassured her that she was on time and everything was okay with me.

Then I said to her, I guess I better introduce myself. I'm Sandra Tucker. Call me Sandy. I think you will enjoy working here I told her. I wanted her to feel welcomed and needed!

Then I told her that we were all glad to have her as part of the team here at Fancy Hair & Manicures. We are all like family here, best friends!! If you have any questions or problems, or need help in any way, don't hesitate to ask. We all are here for you.

By this time all of the other girls had came and gathered around Amber to welcome her to the salon. Everyone was saying hello and welcoming Amber all at the same time! It sounded like a bunch of wild chickens squawking. When all the noise quieted, I pointed to each employee as I began to tell Amber who they all were.

I said to Amber, that Pam, the one that greeted you at the door, Meagan, and Carolyn are my hair washers and also do make-up. Carolyn also styles hair. Anita and Patricia are my stylist and masseuses. Tammy, she does just about anything that involves the hair, nails, face and skin. Tammy hates to do the toes though, I said with a laugh!

I told Amber that Tammy had been the one filling in for the manicure specialist that had just left us. I told her that Tammy would be working along side of her. I said to her that once she got into her groove she'd have it all to herself. But until then, Tammy would be at her beckon call whenever she needed her.

I told Amber about how Tammy was what we called the floater around the salon. I told her that Tammy helps everyone with their jobs and even when we need a little time off Tammy would fill in if she could. She's our little Angel!!!

Then I said laughingly, but don't get on her bad side. Tammy is like a cat with her tail on fire if you make her mad. She don't take any crap off anyone!

The girls laughed out at that remark except Amber. I don't know if I scared her, or if she just didn't care either way. Finally the introductions were over.

I then told Tammy to take Amber and show her the area where she'd be stationed. I told the others to get to work as I did myself too.

I had also told Amber that she could arrange things so that she would feel at home. She did just that! I watched as she began moving things around to suit her needs. That made me feel good about her. She appeared a little more confident!

While at my work station, I noticed that Amber was looking at her appointment book. I could see that she was reading the names listed for the day.

One of her scheduled appointments that she had read was "Mystic". I could hear her talking to Tammy about it. Amber knew that Mystic was one of the biggest country music stars of today. She was one of the greats!

Mystic is my idol, Amber stated! I heard her say to Tammy that Mystic had made it big with the song called "Play Crazy"! Apparently Amber knew her idol very well.

I heard Amber ask Tammy; is this for real! Yes, Tammy had told her. She was so excited but also she seemed scared to death! What if "Ms. Mystic" didn't like her? What if she messed up? With all the excitement, you couldn't help but overhear Amber as she was rattling on to Tammy.

I went over to Amber. I cut her off and said you'll be just fine. I hired you because of your work ethics. I told her that Mystic was a regular around here and so were a lot of other celebrities. You'll get used to it, I told her. They are people just like us. They put one pant leg on at a time, and they also pass gas too!!!!

Everyone had heard what I had said and laughed out. All except Amber. I guess she didn't think those remarks were very funny!

I didn't care. There was always a lot of humor here at the salon! We were all just plain ole southerners. Common folks! There was always someone making jokes or something funny was always happening! It was never a dull moment!

As excited as Amber seemed about her celebrity clients and the way she was rattling on to Tammy about it, I thought maybe she wasn't so shy after all. I thought maybe she was just worried that she might have not gotten the job if she thought she had been late. Maybe she had to just loosen up!

I watched Amber throughout the morning. The way Amber was carrying on, you'd thought she had known Tammy all her life. I guess Tammy must have made Amber feel right at home. Amber seemed more relaxed. Even though Tammy was a hell cat when she was mad, she was a friendly sweet person otherwise.

Later on about mid morning I heard the door chimes to the salon entrance. The chimes had been chiming since 8:00am. I looked around toward the door and saw that it was Mystic.

When Mystic came in, she just spoke out and said Hey ya'll! I'm here to get my nails done. Mystic had a southern accent like no other!

Then Mystic said, ya'll know I'm a nail biter and I ain't got very much more nails left to bite! I need all the help I can get, and she just kept rattling on!

I looked over at Amber. She was white as a ghost. I thought Amber was going to faint right where she stood!

I went over and greeted Mystic and whispered to her that this was Amber's first day, but assured her that Amber would do her the best set of nails she'd ever had.

I turned and walked away and said under my breath, God I hope she does! I thought to myself, up to this point of the morning there hadn't been any complaints. Amber had done very well so far!

Amber didn't faint! Mystic had made it easy for Amber and after a few minutes Amber seemed to have relaxed again. She did Mystic's manicure so beautiful. I watched Amber as she worked on Mystic's nails. She was a professional! Mystic had even tipped Amber fifty bucks. I saw Mystic when she had passed the tip into Amber's hand as she got up from the manicure chair to leave.

When Mystic headed toward the door to leave she held up her hands to show off her new set of nails. As she passed by me, she slipped a hand full of concert tickets into my hand and then said see ya'll next week.

Then Mystic said, Sandy, you've got a winner there, but I think she's a little nutsy, but aint we all and then she laughed! Then out the door she went.

I was glad that Amber didn't hear that remark from Mystic. I would have hated for her to leave the job position before she had got started good!

After Mystic had left we thought that Amber was going to need CPR. Amber went on once again to tell all of us that Mystic was one of her idols. Amber's hands trembled as she spoke of Mystic! Amber gasps for air a time or two as she spoke!

She continued to talk about Mystic for most of the day it seemed. That shy girl that had come in earlier wasn't shy anymore!

At one time during the morning I had heard Amber singing to one of Mystic's song that had been playing on the radio that we had on at the salon. She sounded pretty good too.

At some time before lunch I went over to Amber's work station. I said to her that I'd heard her singing. I told Amber I'd have to take her to a little family dance over in Trina Alabama. It's a place just across the state line. It's called the Rancher's Dance Barn I told her!

I said to her that my boyfriend Jerry Haggard played music over there whenever he came in from his road tours. I'd also told her, I was sure that he wouldn't mind if she got up and sung with the band. He lets many guest come and sing.

Amber laughed. She said she used to sing with a band when she was younger. She said it sounded like fun and she'd like to go sometimes. She then asks me who Jerry Haggard was. She'd never heard of him!

I said to her, I'll have to tell you about him at another time. We were just to busy to get into that conversation at the time. I told her to ask me about him later. She said she would!

The morning had passed by quickly. Business had slowed! It was lunch time. I was starving. We all were starving! We all decided to order out for pizza.

Once the pizza order had been called in, Tammy took orders for cold drinks for all of us. She said she would run across the street to the gas station to get our drinks while we waited on the pizza to arrive. Tammy had come back with the drinks along with candy bars, snack cakes and packs of crackers. Tammy must have really been starving! I ask her did she buy the store out! We all laughed!

Tammy had went to everyone and handed each one their drink and the snacks. The pizza had arrived. I locked the door to the salon and we began feasting on the pizza and snacks.

Amber ate very quietly at her work station. We had asked her to come and sit with us in the break room. She said "I'm fine here"! She said she wanted to look over her appointment book.

She had seemed to let her shyness return. I wondered how she could be so involved and then be so distant. It was like she had a split personality. Maybe Mystic was right. Maybe she was a nut!

I didn't care. She had impressed Mystic! She had done excellent manicures all morning and that was all that mattered to me! I hoped that she would impress others as they came into the salon during the remainder of the day! In the future too!

The rest of us had a great time during our lunch break. We talked about how Amber was doing and everyone seemed to think she would work out fine! Lunch was soon over. We cleaned our mess, and I unlocked the door to the salon. It was back to work.

Amber did another customer's nails. Another satisfied client! Amber was really great at her job!

As soon as Amber had finished with the satisfied client she came over to me and said she didn't have another appointment for the next half hour. She said she needed to take her car and put gas in it. She asks if I'd care if she went to the station and filled her gas tank. She knew the station would be closed before we closed the salon. She said she would be back quickly. She said she wanted to drive around after work to sightsee the beautiful hills of Tennessee.

I said for her to go ahead and take her time. It was no need to be in a hurry I told her. We are pretty casual around here. I laughed and said I'm not a slave driver! Now get out of here!

With that being said, Amber went and grabbed her wallet and car keys and headed out the door.

No sooner than Amber could get out the door, Tammy came to me and told me of an unusual happening. She seemed so upset, that we didn't take time to go into the conference room!

Tammy said that she had caught Amber throwing the pack of crackers she'd given her in the garbage. She said she had watched Amber rip open the pack and crumble the crackers in her hand and dump them in the trash can!! She said Amber didn't know she had been seen doing this.

I told Tammy; maybe the crackers were stale or out of date. Tammy was getting pretty fired up! She said hers weren't stale! Tammy was mad because she had spent her own money to buy the crackers that Amber had trashed. It wasn't that the money mattered, but the fact that Amber had just thrown the crackers away without saying a word about it. She could have given them to someone else, she said! Tammy was really pissed off!

Tammy was going to confront Amber! I ask her, begged her not to say anything. Tammy, being the hot head she is, I didn't want Amber to get scared off and leave the job I needed filled.

I told Tammy to let me handle it! Tammy agreed not to say anything to Amber, but she sure didn't like it.

About fifteen minutes had gone by. Amber returned. I looked over at Tammy and she nodded to assure me she wouldn't say anything.

I stopped Amber as she was headed to her work station. I ask Amber if she'd gotten her gas tank filled and if everything was alright? She said yes to both questions. Nothing was said about the cracker incident at this time.

I thought to myself; I'd talk to Amber about the cracker incident later. Now wasn't the time. Amber returned to her work station and was waiting on her next client. Amber acted as if nothing had happened!

A few minutes later I watched as Tammy excused herself from Amber. Then Tammy made a bee line to the outside store front! I went out to follow Tammy. When I got outside Tammy was pacing back and forth on the concrete and mumbling to herself!

I told Tammy to keep cool about everything. I told her I'd get with Amber about the crackers before closing! I told her to calm down before she came back inside. I assured her everything would be alright!

I turned and went back inside to do my next client's hair. Tammy soon followed. You couldn't have cut the tension with a knife!

Finally it was 6:00 pm. It was closing time! Everything went pretty well for that first day I had thought! Why was I so concerned this morning? The clients loved Amber! The other workers loved her. There was not the first complaint! Except that Tammy saw Amber trashing some crackers she had purchased! Maybe Amber Lynn Newby was the right choice. I hollered okay girls, let's close up shop!

Each one started closing there work station. I said to them, shouting loudly, another great day!! Thanks to each of you!! Right then and there, I gave thanks to God for making everything work out. I thanked him out loud too!

Amber just looked at me like I was crazy. All the other employees had seen me get a little "CRAZY" they called it, from time to time, so they went on with what they were doing. They were ready to go home. I was too. With things in order for closing, we all hauled out of the salon and I locked the door behind me.

Everyone was heading to their vehicles. Then I thought oh my goodness, I didn't speak to Amber about the crackers! I hollered at Tammy before she'd gotten inside her car. She turned and walked over to me. I told her that I didn't get the chance to speak to Amber about the crackers. I reassured her that I would talk to Amber the next day!

Tammy said it didn't matter. She had gotten over it! Then Tammy said to me, maybe those crackers were stale! She told me not to bother Amber about it!

With Tammy satisfied, I went to my car and got in and started it. Just as I began to drive off I remembered that I needed to stop by the grocery store. I wanted to pick up a few things before heading home.

With it being nearly 50 miles between the city of Brownsboro Tennessee where I worked, and the county of Michelle Tennessee where I lived, and the only store that was anywhere close to my place was 10 miles away and that store didn't stock some of the things I needed, I sure didn't want to go back out once I got home.

It was times like this that I wondered why I shouldn't just sale my home and get a place closer to the salon. But

I'd been making that same drive for 18 years! Why change anything now!

I got to the grocery store and went inside. The grocery store seemed busy. I whizzed around gathering the things I needed. I guess I had been in the store about 10 minutes. I had gotten a loaf of bread, some banana's, a gallon of milk, a box of crackers and a bag of donuts.

I was headed toward the check out line and nearly ran over the grocery cart of Amber's. Amber was coming out from an isle stocked with canned goods. We both were saying excuse me at the same time. I guess neither of us was paying attention to where we were going!

We spoke briefly about her day at the salon which was mostly about Mystic. Amber said she felt really welcome and had a lot of fun. Nowhere else had she ever worked that she felt loved she said. I said well that's great. I guess we made a pretty good first impression for your first day!

Amber then noticed my grocery cart of foods and remarked about the crackers. She said something like crackers made her sick! She didn't mention anything about the other things in my cart. She hated crackers she said.

I thought, now is a good time to ask why she hated crackers? Maybe her answer would explain the incident at the salon. I ask why she hated crackers and she said just that her mother fed them to her a lot when she was younger.

While Amber was telling me this, she seemed to get teary eyed. After seeing her expression, I guessed they must have been poor and that's what they ate most of the time. Maybe that's why she had thrown away the crackers earlier at the salon. I guessed crackers were a sad reminder of her past. I just couldn't question her any further about the incident!

Anyway, Amber quickly changed the subject back to her first day at the salon. We spoke a few more minutes and I finally said that I better get going before it got to dark for me to see to drive. I told her about the long drive I had ahead of me and said I'd see her tomorrow! I went through the check out line and then left for home.

CHAPTER 4

THE SLEEPOVER

The next day at the salon everyone was on time. It was another busy day! I was doing a cut and style on one of our Tennessee residents.

Patricia was doing a massage on Mr. Thompson whom was a regular client. Meagan was doing a client's make up and had another client waiting. Carolyn was styling a client's hair.

Pam was washing the hair of a client. She had the well known "Angel Wings" hair in her hands! Angel Wings was known for her work nationwide in helping get food to hungry children all over the world. She was given the name Angel Wings because people felt she was an angel sent by God and that without wings she couldn't deliver to the needy.

Anita was giving a massage to a famous male singer songwriter, Rex Marlin, of the country band called "BANDANA".

Tammy was helping Amber, and vise versa, as they were lined up with clients waiting! Even though they were covered up with clients, Amber seemed even more relaxed than she had been the previous day.

Amber did the nails for Maria Gordon. Maria was the wife of the famous Violinist, Don Gordon. Amber also did a pedicure and manicure for Bridgett Jones. Bridgett was a famous female racecar driver. Amber was doing great work. She was getting really great comments from all the clients. Nothing strange happened.

I briefly had gotten the chance to tell Tammy about the grocery store scene I had with Amber! Tammy didn't seem to let the wasted cracker incident get in her way of Amber and her working side by side. Surprisingly, Tammy seemed to actually like Amber. It was as if Tammy felt sorry for Amber in a way. As each day passed Amber got more and more relaxed and all of us loved her. She seemed to fit in so well!

Another few weeks had passed by. Amber was a joy to have around. Still a little shy, but she had a way that made you care for her deeply.

Amber was working by herself now. She didn't need Tammy's help. Tammy was thrilled to be back to her floater position. I was too! Tammy was a great deal of help to all of us!

On a Saturday, I was finishing a perm on one of my clients. It was almost closing time. It was my last fix for the day.

After the client had left I went over to Amber. I told Amber that once every couple of months or so, all of us at the salon got together at my house for a girls sleep over. All of us except Patricia! Amber knew that Patricia had a husband and two children to care for. Just on occasion sometimes Patricia would come by the house and hang out for an hour or two, but she never did sleep over.

Tonight was the night I said to Amber. No boyfriends allowed. No booze allowed. I told her that we watched movies, ate all kinds of junk foods, and we would fix each others hair, trying unusual styles. I told her that we do each others nails and just hang out together to have a fun fellowship together.

I told her we all wanted her to come. Amber seemed happy for the invite! She said she would be there.

I gave her directions to my house. After closing the salon for the day I went home. I straightened the house some before everyone would arrive. I made sure that I had set out plenty of food and snacks for everyone.

The first to arrive was Tammy. She came early to see if I needed help with anything before everyone arrived. After assuring Tammy everything was ready, she and I went to the kitchen table and talked while waiting on the others.

It was at this time that Tammy and I had talked a bit more about Amber and the thing with the crackers! Tammy and I agreed that something must have happened in Ambers past with crackers but we just didn't know what it was!

As we were talking, we heard a knock at the door. Tammy and I got up and went to greet the guest. It was Pam and Meagan. They came inside and before we all could get sat down the door was being knocked upon again. It was Anita and Carolyn.

We opened the door and let them in. We were all waiting for Amber to get there! We had gathered into my living room. Setting around chatting, finally another knock on the door. It was Amber.

We all greeted her at the door and invited her inside. She had a small overnight bag in her hand. I told her she could put it anywhere she wanted. She set her bag at the end of the couch next to the other overnight bags that had been brought in.

Everyone was talking at once. Everyone was glad to see Amber had come! Now everyone had arrived. It was eight pm. We were having a really fun time.

We had created a new hair design. We all decided that Tammy would get to display the new creation on Monday morning when we all returned to work. Tammy would try anything. She was the dare devil!

We had even given Amber a new hair design also. I told Amber that she should keep it that way! I told her she didn't look as tom boyish with it like that! I don't think she liked that remark, but it was too late to take it back! It had already been said!

The time had passed by quickly. We had done each others hair and nails. We did facials on each other. Amber didn't like the make up on her face! The rest of us thought she looked rather pretty with make up on! We joked around and were acting silly. We basically had a pillow fight with make-up! We watched a two hour movie and stuffed ourselves with junk food.

It was late. Me being the old lady of the bunch and being that I was sleepy, I told the girls I was going to bed. I told them they could stay up all night if they wanted to but I needed my beauty sleep! It was already after midnight. I went to bed.

CHAPTER 5

AMBER MOVES IN

I was the first to wake up early Sunday morning after the long night. It was about 7:30am. I crawled out of bed and headed toward the kitchen.

I approached the living room. The TV was blasting loudly! The girls were scattered all over the place.

From an adjoining room off from the living room I saw that one of the girls had taken a spare bedroom. I wondered how in the world they got in the room, for the room was piled high with clothing and blankets. The other girls were piled in the living room floor. They had blankets covering them. All you could see was their head sticking out! I had to step over them. One girl was on the sofa covered up to her neck.

I went on into the kitchen. I put on a pot of coffee. It wasn't long before the coffee had finished making.

I was setting at the kitchen table having my coffee and a cigarette. I guess I'd already smoked a cigarette or two. I'd lost count on the cups of coffee I'd consumed. I was starring at the mess we all had created the night before.

I heard footsteps coming toward the kitchen. It was now somewhere around 8:00am. It was Amber that came dragging in, yawning like there was no tomorrow. Her hair was standing up all over her head and was a terrible mess!

I offered her a cup of coffee but she reached in the fridge and got a soda instead. She sat down at the table.

Amber stretched her arms out and yawned again. Amber said I've never had so much fun! Say you guys get together every couple of months like this. I said yeah! She said I don't think I could stand this much fun any more often than that!!! I said yeah, me too!!!

Amber then commented about the mess we all had made and the next thing I knew, she was up cleaning it. I told her to leave it be and that I'd clean it later but she insisted on cleaning it up. Besides she said that's a small price to pay for that kind of fun and that bed I slept in!

I then said to Amber; so you were the one that got lucky and beat the others to the spare bedroom?

She said yes. She said when she had decided to go to sleep; everyone else was still wide open. She grabbed the first bedroom she came to and flopped right onto the bed. She had dumped the piles of clothing and blankets that were on the bed onto the floor. Before she knew it she was asleep, she said.

Then Amber said; I can't remember the last time that I slept on a real bed. I said to her "you don't have a bed at your place"?

She said, Well, to tell you the truth, I haven't been able to find a place yet. Motel rooms are too expensive! I've been parking my car behind the salon and sleeping in it. I purchased a membership at the gym across the street just so I could use the showers, and it doesn't hurt me any to use the treadmill too. I'll find a place soon I'm sure.

I couldn't believe what I had just heard! Amber had been sleeping in her car for over a month. Right then and there, I told her to bring her things back here to my home later in the afternoon and she was staying here with me. She resisted, but I insisted! Amber finally said ok. She continued to clean!

It wasn't long before everyone was up and lollygagging around my kitchen. I was still setting at the kitchen table in my old pajamas drinking coffee and smoking another cigarette.

As I looked around at everyone, I began to laugh hysterically! Someone said to me, what's so funny! I said just take a look around! I said oh my Lord, I could get arrested! I said if the cops came and knocked on my door and saw the sight in my kitchen, they'd swear I was running a whore house!

Everyone except Amber began to laugh! They saw what I was talking about! Meagan, with her brick house build was leaning across the kitchen counter. Her chiffon night gown was showing off her assets as she leaned across the counter.

Across from me sat Tammy. She had on a tiny white satin baby doll night gown that showed off her petite body. Her breast was in full view as she leaned over the kitchen table.

The other girls were dressed similar and had body parts exposed except for Amber. She had on an over sized t-shirt and pajama pants. Nothing was showing but her bare feet.

All the girls except Amber and myself began to dance around the kitchen. They were laughing and joking around!

Things got more seriously funny when I heard Anita say to Meagan as if Meagan was a cop, please, please arrest me Mr. Cop! Anita was prancing around Meagan and flirting with her as if she was a man!

Again everybody was laughing! All but Amber. She didn't seem to take part in what was going on as everyone else did. She didn't seem to think it was very funny. She wasn't laughing anyway!

Amber just continued to clean. She was washing dishes at the sink while all the clowning was going on. I sat at the table laughing my head off at the girls!

Finally the clowning around stopped and everyone was serious again. Everyone began cleaning up the mess and before we knew it everything was back in order. I remarked to the girls that the place hadn't been that clean before anyone had arrived on Saturday night before the sleep over!

It was nearly lunch time. We had passed breakfast time without even realizing it. I told everyone we could fix a burger or something if they were hungry. Nobody was hungry.

I think everyone was to worn out to think about eating. Everybody began to gather their belongings and they had gotten dressed and prepared to leave.

Soon everyone had left. I went and set at the kitchen table. I drank more coffee. One cup after another. A cigarette in hand with each cup. I got to thinking about Amber. Why hadn't she said something about having to live in her car? Embarrassed maybe? Pride?

The time was slipping away. As usual, my mind was going 90 miles an hour! Amber would be back here soon with her things. Even though everyone had cleaned my home before leaving, there were a few things that I wanted to do before Amber returned.

I put out my cigarette and got up from the kitchen table to get things done. I went into the spare bedroom I had. I would have it ready for Amber when she arrived. The room had its own bath and a walk in closet. I figured that the closet would give her enough room to store her things.

Sharing a bathroom wouldn't be a good idea either since we would probably be running over each other while getting ready for work each morning.

I put clean towels out and put fresh sheets on the bed. I went out to my flower garden and gathered a bouquet of flowers. I put them in a vase with water and placed them on the bedside table. It would brighten up the room.

I removed clothes from the closet. They were just some old winter clothes. I had used that closet and room mostly for storage. I ran the vacuum over the carpet. I dusted the furniture.

I had just finished with the room and walked into the living room to set down when I heard a knock at the door. I knew it had to be Amber. I wasn't expecting anyone else.

I went to the door and looked through the peep hole. It was Amber. I opened the door to let her in. Once she was inside, she kept saying "are you sure you want to do this for me".

I assured her "I did". I said, come on. I'll show you your room I have fixed for you. I took Amber to the room. She said she loved it and that it was perfect. She was so graciously thankful. Then I gave her a spare house key so that she could come and go as she pleased.

By this time we had went to the kitchen. I ask was she hungry? She said she was! As we talked to each other I started cooking up some food. I was hungry too!

I told Amber that it was always quiet here. I never had much company to come visit. I told her the only time she would hear anyone come around, was if Jerry was in off the road. I told her that he traveled for weeks at a time. I told her that any other time anyone was around was pretty much whenever we had the sleepovers.

While I was cooking and Amber was standing watching me cook, she noticed a picture on my refrigerator door. She pointed to the picture and asks me who the good looking hunk was in it?

I told her the picture was of Jerry. He was good looking all dressed in his cowboy cut blue jeans with the creases sewn in, a western tailored shirt that showed off his muscular build and his cowboy hat that covered his gorgeous head of dark brown hair. His skin was the dark rich color of a farmers' tan. An extremely good looking man to be forty four years old! I quickly let Amber know that he was my fellow!

Amber then began asking me questions about Jerry and what he did for a living. She said, I remember you saying he played music in Alabama. I've never heard of him she said. What kind of music does he play? She had a lot of questions.

Once she stopped talking, I began answering her, as we both got our food into plates and set at the table to eat. I started by telling her that Jerry was a really great guy. Amber seemed very interested in knowing about him. I told her how I'd met him about four years ago at a dance in Alabama. A place called the Ranchers Dance Barn. I said to her; do you remember the dance I had told you about before!

I told her that I had just lost my mother to a stroke back then. A few of the girls from the salon had taken me at this dance to help me not to think about my mother's death.

On that particular night at the dance, Jerry was on the stage singing and playing his guitar. Amber was eagerly listening! She wanted to know more!

I went on. I told Amber that he sings and plays the old honky tonk style music. He doesn't care for the new country, I told her! He was and still is so talented. Anyway, the girls introduced me to him and we've been together ever since.

I told Amber about how Jerry and I would see each other between the gigs he had booked and whenever he played over at the Rancher's Dance Hall. I told her how he'd gotten many offers to make it big in the business but had turned them down. He's always wanted to do things like he wanted. He doesn't want anyone telling him how or what to do! I told her how he books his own gigs from town to town and that he can come and go as he pleases.

Then I told Amber again, that the next time Jerry was in Alabama I'd take her to hear him play. She said to me that that would be fun! She said she could hardly wait to hear him and his band!

The evening had passed by quickly. Amber and I had finished eating the food I had prepared. Amber grabbed up our plates and proceeded to clear the table of what was left of our meal. She cleaned the dishes as I dried them and put them away.

After we finished the dishes, Amber and I sat and talked for a short while longer. We mostly talked about music. I was beginning to get sleepy.

I told Amber that I was going to bed. I told her that I was going to Church the next morning. I invited her to go with me. She didn't seem too interested! She didn't refuse, but she also didn't except. She just said for me to ask her again in the morning.

Morning came and as I suspected, Amber didn't go to Church with me. That was okay though. I didn't force Church on anyone! I just felt it was my duty to invite. You know, you have to open the door and leave it open, but you can't make anyone come in if they don't want too! God knows, I have missed Church more times than I'd like to admit! I was surely not one to judge!

As the days passed Amber and I were getting along pretty good. We didn't seem to get in each others way. We drove our own cars to work each day. We fixed our own breakfast! Sometimes we ate together. We had the bathroom time down like clockwork! Even though she had her own bath in her room, we had to have a set time as to when to bathe or one of us would have to take a cold one. So far, it had worked out great! We always had plenty of hot water!

We both had our alone time and our together time. We pretty much did what ever we wanted without interfering with the other.

One afternoon Amber mentioned the concert tickets that "Mystic" had given me. I had forgotten about them. I went and retrieved them from my work bag. I gave them to Amber. I told her that I wasn't going to be able to go.

I suggested that she could get some of the girls at work to go with her. I knew they would love to go see "Mystic"! Amber begged for me to go with her. I just can't, I told her! I had other things to take care of.

Amber didn't seem to like the fact that I wouldn't go with her. She seemed to take it personal, or at least that's what I was reading from her. Finally, she gave up trying to get me to go along.

The day came for the concert. It ended up that Amber and Tammy went to the show by themselves. The other tickets were wasted. It was after midnight when Amber arrived home from the concert. She had awakened me by making noise in her room.

I thought that Amber might try to come into my bedroom and want to talk about the concert. Hoping that she wouldn't, and that I was tired, I just lay quietly until I realized that Amber had gone to bed herself. Finally I dozed off back to sleep.

While at work the next day, Amber couldn't quit talking about how great the concert was! Once again, she rattled on to me about how she idolized Mystic. She had seemed to have forgotten that she was upset with me for not going to the concert with her.

Another couple of months had gone. Summer time had arrived. It was hot and muggy outside. The air conditioner in the salon was running full blast. It felt good to walk into the salon and feel the cool air in your face.

Even though it was a hot and humid time, we were almost always busy during this time of year. You would think that business would slow down due to the heat. Hair didn't do so well with this kind of humidity.

The majority of appointments were for manicures and pedicures though. That was good for Amber. She got to meet a bunch of celebrities and plenty of Tennessee residents. With the walk-ins and scheduled appointments Amber was totally covered up almost every day. Tammy was helping her out as much as possible.

Amber had made a couple of friends outside the salon. Yeah, Amber Lynn was working out just great! Not only at the salon but also at my home. She helped with so many things!

She did most of the chores. She insisted! She cleaned, did the laundry, ran errands, and just about everything else.

The cooking we shared. We would both be in the kitchen trying out new recipes, making the biggest mess you ever saw. It was always a lot of fun.

It was also kind of nice to have someone around just to talk to and I guessed I was a good listener for her too.

We would set in the living room on the couch and talk for hours. I learned so much about Amber Lynn during these talks.

I already knew that we had the same birth date from when I saw it in her resume when I had hired her. I was just the oldest. I was ten years older!

Amber's father had died when she was only three years old. Her mother had raised her until she ran away from home at the age of fifteen. Amber hated crackers. That's what she had said that day at the grocery store. And still to this day I hadn't questioned Amber's reason for trashing the crackers that day at the salon.

Amber still doesn't know that Tammy had seen her trashing those crackers nor does she know that Tammy had told me about it. I didn't want to embarrass her by saying anything. If Amber felt the need to talk about it sometimes later, then I would be here to listen.

I learned that Amber had lived her teen years on the streets. She had been in gangs, on drugs and booze. She had stolen and had been a prostitute. She told me she had to survive somehow!

When Amber turned 21, she was old enough to go into bars. She said she spent a lot of time in them because she drank a lot.

She told me about a time that one night while at a club; a bartender heard her singing along with a band that was playing. She usually sat at the bar, she had told me. The bartender had gone to the band leader and before she new it, she was up on the stage singing. The crowd loved her. They must have been pretty drunk she had said, laughing!

The band ended up hiring her. She eventually quit drinking and got off the drugs. She loved music so much. That was her "high" she'd said!

When Amber turned 22, she decided to do more with her life. She went to school and got her degree in cosmetology. With what money she had made at the clubs singing at night on weekends, plus taking on a part time job at a laundry mat working a few days a week paid for her to go to school. She had taken cosmetology night classes thru the week. She said she didn't get a lot of sleep back then!

She told me it had taken her two years to complete her courses. She was 25 years old when she got her first job in a salon. She said she had done hair back then, but her preference was doing the nails. She eventually became a professional manicure specialist.

That's why I had hired her. I needed the best. Amber was now 29 years young. Amber and I agreed that she has a good future with my salon if she chose to stick around.

CHAPTER 6

TRYING TO FIT IN

The summer had quickly passed by right before my eyes. Amber had become one of us! She was like family! She had experienced another sleepover.

Amber had gone on a picnic with us. Although she came along for the picnic, Amber spent most of the picnic time by herself. She would just set on the banks of the waters edge all alone. If someone walked down to the water to speak to Amber or invite her to come join in a game of volley ball or some other game we played, she'd say she just wanted to set and watch the water.

Amber had finally attended a church service with me. I had tried many times to get her to go back with me. She refused!

She had gone skating with us girls, but she had quickly left not long after she had arrived. She made the statement she was tired and was going home.

With the way Amber was acting, I was beginning to think she was jealous. She didn't seem to like it when others were around me. She always wanted me to do things with her and no one else. Once she had said to me, as if she was a little girl, why does Carolyn always have to hang around us?

I didn't see anything wrong with Carolyn being with us I said to her. She didn't say anything after that. She just seemed to pout!

Time went by. My suspicions of Amber were becoming a reality. Not only did she seem jealous but Amber was becoming very possessive! Me, I loved being around people. Lot's of them I'd tell her!

I remember one Saturday night when Jerry was taking a break from the road. He was coming to my house to spend some time with me. I hadn't seen him for several months. We had talked almost every day by telephone though.

Amber had told me she was going out for the night with her new found friend Julie. This I thought would work out great! Jerry and I would have the place to ourselves!

Just after Amber had left the house to be with her friend Julie, I heard a motorcycle. I looked out my window. It was Jerry. I watched as he pulled that huge cycle into the drive. I ran out to greet him.

He had barely gotten off the motorcycle and had removed his helmet when I gave him a bear hug and kissed him. He returned hugs and kisses.

As we walked arm in arm going into my house and Jerry with his guitar strapped on his back, I ask him where he got the Harley. How have you been? I sure have missed you, I told him! He was answering me as fast as I could ask questions!

Now inside my house, Jerry and I had been enjoying each others company for a couple of hours. He had serenaded me with his guitar and had sung a song or two for me. I even sang along with him. He says I sing pretty good! I guess I'm not too bad!

Then we were sharing ice cream. We were cuddled up together on the sofa when Amber had come in. Jerry and I were watching TV. Amber walked over toward us and said what are ya'll doing?

I said something to her like we're just hanging out. I introduced Jerry to Amber. I then said to Amber, we haven't had an opportunity to be by ourselves for a long time!

Amber began to make small talk! She'd never met Jerry in person before. She said to Jerry, I know who you are! I saw your picture on Sandy's refrigerator! She continued to speak about things that didn't seem to matter! She didn't seem to care or get the hint that we wanted to be alone.

Amber just kept standing there! I ask Amber what happened to her night out with her friend. She said something to the effect of "oh, Julie had to meet with her sister down at the grill". They were going to have burgers and then go visit with an aunt"!

Amber then said "I didn't want to interfere with their plans so I came home"! In my mind I was thinking "what about my plans" but I didn't say anything.

Amber then started acted as if the TV show that Jerry and I had been watching had caught her interest. Jerry was such a nice guy that he finally ask Amber if she wanted to watch TV with us. She said sure and she plopped herself down over in a chair.

I knew she was settled there for the rest of the night! I could tell by the way Amber looked at me that she didn't like it that Jerry was near me.

No, Amber wasn't gay! She just seemed to get an attitude about her when I was with or around anyone other than her. Amber was like that with everyone! It had to be just her and one other! She didn't like to share!

I guessed that's why she came home this particular night! She didn't want to share her new friend Julie with anyone! Not even her friend's sister or aunt!

As Jerry and I were snuggled up together on the sofa, Amber seemed to be trying everything she could to keep me and Jerry apart.

At one point Amber had gotten up and went to the kitchen. While in there, I heard her call my name a couple of times. Eventually Amber succeeded to get me to come to the kitchen. She said she was looking for the creamer for her coffee and couldn't find it! It was in plain sight on the counter!

Another attempt, Amber had gone to her bedroom for a blanket. She couldn't find one! She hollered at me to come and help her look for it. I went to her room. There it is I told her! The blanket was in the top of her closet! I knew she had to have seen it. She was a whole lot taller than I was and I spotted the blanket as soon as I walked into her room!

After that incident, we were back into the living room and I had settled back into Jerry's arms.

Amber then decided she wanted to talk about stuff! And she did! We couldn't watch TV without Amber asking questions about Jerry's music or wanting to talk about something to do with the salon.

Jerry didn't seem to let it bother him that Amber was there! He just did what ever he felt like doing. If he wanted to kiss me, he did! If he wanted to wrestle with me or tickle me, he did! And even though Jerry was a nice guy and answered Amber's questions, I began to wonder if Jerry was doing things just to piss Amber off! If so, it was working! Eventually, Amber ended up excusing herself and going to her bedroom.

The night was still young. With the movie that we had tried to watch on TV being over with, Jerry and I decided to go take a ride on his motor cycle.

As we left the house and proceeded to climb onto his motor cycle, I noticed Amber looking out her bedroom window. Her bedroom light was on. I could see her from the front lawn of my house.

I guess Amber must have seen me looking at her. I saw her turn away! I could see Ambers arm raise as she threw something across the room! What was wrong with that girl! I didn't understand Amber!

As Jerry and I were taking off on his motor cycle, I again turned toward her window. I saw Amber looking out her window once again. I wondered about Amber but I wasn't going to let her ruin my night with Jerry!

The motorcycle ride was so much fun. We rode around the country roads as I wrapped my arms around Jerry's waist. We kissed at every intersection that we had stopped at. It was good to be back into Jerry's arms again. I missed him so much when he was away.

We ended the night with a dinner out and then Jerry taking me home. After a goodbye kiss, Jerry headed back on the road.

Thank goodness that Amber was asleep when I got home. I didn't feel up to talking. I just wanted to go to sleep and have wonderful thoughts and dreams about Jerry. That's just what I did. I surely didn't want to deal with Amber and her strangeness.

As I continue my story, I must tell you of another time that Amber had acted strangely! It was on a Sunday. I had just arrived home from church. It was pouring down rain! Amber had come from her bedroom as I entered my home.

She stated to me that she had made lunch if I was hungry. I began to say to her that I was starving! I was saying to her that I would eat after I had changed out of my Sunday clothes. Then I had asked her what she had cooked? All this time I had my back to her as I was speaking. I was removing my shoes at the door. I didn't want to track mud on my floor from where I'd accidentally stepped in a mud puddle before entering the house.

Amber didn't respond to my question! I turned to where Amber had been standing and she had vanished! She had walked off while I was talking to her! I knew she had heard me talking to her. I wondered where she had gone off to! I got my shoes off and then went toward my bedroom to change my clothes.

Amber came from out of her bedroom as I was going to mine. She startled me! I then ask her again "what did you cook"?

She remarked to me that she'd heard me the first time! You'll just have to go see for yourself, she said! I just shook my head in confusion! This wasn't the first time Amber had done a disappearing act while she was being spoken to!

I wondered how someone could make you care about them so much and then make you crazy with their ways and personality. Other than Amber's strangeness, she was precious to me! She had fit in just as my former employer Jamie had!

CHAPTER 7

AMBER SINGS WITH THE BAND

At the salon we were always celebrating something! Whether it was a new baby; someone getting engaged; birthdays or an anniversary. Heck, we would just celebrate because we had a good month at work!

It was Amber's 6th month anniversary working here at the salon. Had it been that long? Time had gone by so fast.

It was the most beautiful time of the year. It was the beginning of autumn. The leaves on the trees were beginning to change colors. Their presence gave me a sense of peace. The golden and red/orange colors of the leaves that flowed to the ground looked like a bed as they piled up around the base of the trees and along the road sides. It was always a pretty sight to see!

Amber was doing so well with her job! She was also still living at my home, but that was okay. She could stay as long as she needed. Though she had been a little weird and strange at times, she had become a good friend.

She was paying way more than her share. Not just by paying on the utilities and groceries, but by doing so much around the place and being a companion. I trusted her totally. She was like a little sister I never had. I would give my life for her.

Anyway, all of us from the salon had decided to surprise Amber with a small party for her 6 months of accomplishments.

We set a date for October 12. It would be on a Saturday during work hours. The day soon arrived and everything went as planned. We opened the salon as scheduled. All through the day we snacked on finger foods and such in between working on our clientele.

We gave Amber gifts of nail polish, shampoos and such. She was totally surprised. She said nobody had ever done anything like that for her. She hugged everyone. She said she was so happy here.

While at the small celebration, I remembered telling Amber about Jerry playing music down in Trina, Alabama. I went over and reminded her about it. She'd only met him the one time at the house and it had been more than a month ago!

I hadn't seen Jerry in over a month either! I said to her, since it was Saturday and we didn't open the salon on Sunday, this would be a perfect time to go.

I told her that she wouldn't get another chance to hear Jerry's band for a few months. He would be back on the road again after the gig over in Alabama! The nearest place he would be playing next would be in Texas.

That also meant that I'd only see him a couple of times for the next few months so I was definitely planning on going to meet him at the dance. I didn't travel to his shows very often. It was always so complicated!

Anyway, when I ask Amber if she'd like to go and hear Jerry's band, she said "Yeah I'll go! It's been a long time since I've been around live music"! It will be fun!

The other girls, my other employee's, heard me talking to Amber about the dance. Everyone from the salon then decided to go.

By the look on Amber's face, you could tell that she didn't like that ideal!

Each one started making their plans to go! Pam and Meagan would bring along their dates. Patricia would have her husband to come along and her two daughters.

Carolyn and Anita would go stag. Their boyfriends couldn't go. Anita's boyfriend worked nights and Carolyn's boyfriends' mother was sick. He had to stay with his mother.

Tammy being a single mom, she would get a baby sitter and come along too! Her son was at the terrible two's stage and she knew she'd be running all over the dance hall just to keep up with him!

Amber then seemed to get excited! How quickly she could change her mind! She wouldn't be the only one without a date she remarked!

Ever since Amber had been living at my house I'd never saw her with a man. She claimed she wasn't ready for a boyfriend. She said she didn't need a man in her life.

Occasionally, she would go out with ONE of us girls if we ask her to, but most times, she would stay at the house. The friends she had made some time back had seemed to have vanished out of her life!

I was always telling her she was too young of a woman to be a home body. I'd tell her, I'll be forty years old soon. Life is to short! I'm not setting home all alone.

Amber knew this about me with out me telling her though! When Jerry was on his tours, I'd usually go out with my girl friends. I didn't stay at home very often.

With the plans made to go to the dance, I was telling the girls I needed something new to wear! I couldn't wear my old worn out jeans! I told them I was going shopping!

Then I thought about Amber! I sure hoped she didn't wear her ole tomboy looking clothes. I didn't even know if she had any stage like clothes to wear should Jerry call her up to sing!

Her work clothes were alright for work but not for the stage! If Jerry called her up to sing, she'd be singing in front of people who would be watching her and those people would be judgmental. People shouldn't be that way, but they are! I didn't want Amber to get embarrassed by anyone!

I began trying to talk Amber into going shopping with me for a new outfit to wear at the dance. I said to her; you and I can leave work at lunch. We'll take the rest of the day off! Tammy will fill in for you! I'm buying, I said! Finally she said she'd go.

Soon it was lunch time, so Amber and I headed out for shopping. We had eaten snacks all morning so we weren't hungry for lunch. We wouldn't have to stop for lunch! That would save us some time and give us more time to shop, I'd told Amber!

As we were in the car, we talked about what she should get to wear. How about a western dress and boots, I said? I told her it would look good on the stage. A little sparkled dress! I wanted her to look feminine. She said "you don't need to spend that kind of money on me"! She said she didn't want to wear a dress. I kept pressuring her. Finally she said okay.

As we went into a couple of clothing shops, at first we found nothing! We shopped for a few hours and finally the last stop, we found the perfect little dress and boots for Amber. She went and tried the outfit on.

When Amber stepped out of the dressing room, WOW, I couldn't believe my eyes! She was just beautiful! I was shocked!

Amber didn't look like a tomboy! I teased that she'd have all the men looking at her! She was acting all shy again. Just as she did when she had first came to work at the salon.

After some convincing Amber agreed on the outfit. With her new outfit and my new jeans, we went back to the salon.

Soon it was time to close up for the day. Before everyone left work, I told them to meet back at the salon and we would all go to the dance in the company van. It would be plenty of room for everyone.

Amber and myself would stay at the salon to get ready for the dance. We didn't have enough time to drive all the way to the house and get dressed and be back in time to leave and not be late for the dance. Trina Alabama was nearly three hours from my home and two hours from the salon! There was no need to backtrack.

With everyone gone, Amber and I began to get ready to go. Amber would say to me, "are you sure this is going to look good"?

I kept saying "Amber you are just beautiful"! Stop worrying! You are going to be the talk of the dance, I bragged! I said to Amber; let me do your make up!

She said she couldn't stand the way make up felt on her face. She had never worn it before. She had tried once to wear it she said but hated it!

After some convincing, Amber let me put make up on her face. Underneath what was a tom boy look before, was a tall slender body that any woman would die for. Along with the make up, Amber looked like a star!

After seeing Amber look so beautiful, I wondered why she had been hiding herself! Lord knows if I looked like that when I was her age I wouldn't hide it!

Now don't get me wrong, I'm not too bad of a looking woman, but I just never had those curves like Amber and some of the other girls have!

Time quickly went by and soon everyone had returned back at the salon. After putting on the finishing touches of lipstick, and each raving about Amber and how pretty she looked, we loaded into the van and headed out.

We were having fun just riding to Alabama. We were making the best of the two hour drive! We remarked about the crazy drivers on the road. There was one old lady who looked to be a hundred years old. She was going so slow. She was doing about 20 in a 60 mile hour zone. We just knew she would get run over someday. I think the little old lady thought she was speeding. I made the statement that that was going to be me one day! Everyone just laughed!

We laughed about the names of the funny road signs we had seen. We laughed at each other. We laughed at Patricia's girls when they said or did something funny!

We listened to the radio and sang along with the singers. Some of us couldn't carry a tune in a tin bucket! But we were having fun!

Amber would seem to just get lost in the music that was coming from the radio. When the "Mystic" song called "Play Crazy" came on the radio, Amber sang every word. It was the number one song of the year! She knew it like the back of her hand. I remember saying to Amber, "come back to the real world".

Finally we saw the road sign that read "Welcome to Trina Alabama". We went about a mile then we could see the huge building up ahead. We were still acting crazy and having fun.

We drove up into the parking lot of the dance hall. You could hear the music outside. The band had already started playing.

We got out of the van and went inside. It looked like a big crowd. Amber was amazed that so many people were at a family dance.

I watched Amber as she moved to the beat of the music while we were paying to enter the dance hall. You could tell that she was really loving everything about this music stuff. She was really into it! You'd thought she was a child at Disney World!

I watched as Patricia's girls were jumping up and down! They were excited! They were patiently waiting to get on the dance floor.

We found a large table that had plenty of chairs that would seat our entire bunch. We had gotten seated, found the restrooms, and the concession stand. Everyone was having a good time!

Amber about had a fit over Jerry's band. They were fantastic she'd say! She said they should be in Nashville recording right beside "Mystic" and the likes!

I reminded Amber that Jerry had been offered so many times to record, but refused. He likes things just the way they are, I had said!

I looked out to the dance floor as it was filled with dancers. I saw that Tammy and Carolyn had made their way to the floor. They were acting foolish! The rest of us were listening to the music and laughing at Tammy and Carolyn.

It wasn't long before I heard Jerry saying over the microphone, "We're gonna take a pause for the cause and we'll be back in fifteen"! The band came off the stage to take a break. Tammy and Carolyn came back to the table.

Jerry came over to our table and set down facing me. He greeted me with a hug and kiss. He asks how I was doing. He said he had missed me! I said "me too"! We talked quietly to each other for a moment or two.

I looked across our table and saw Amber. I ask Jerry if he remembered Amber as I pointed in her direction.

He said yes. He said to Amber, I've heard you can sing? I had already told Jerry about Amber's singing when we had talked on the phone.

She said to him, I'd like to think I can. I know I love to sing! Your band is great she said!

He asks her if she wanted to get up and sing with the band. She said she would be honored to. He told her to be ready. He would call her up after the break.

The band break was over very quick. It was time for Jerry to go back to the stage. I got another kiss as he headed back and he said I love you as he walked away. The band played a song. The dance floor was full once again.

After the song was over and the crowd was headed to their seats I was watching Jerry on stage as he went to the microphone. I knew he was fixing to call on Amber!

Then over the microphone, I heard Jerry announce, we have a guest out there that I've heard is pretty good. Ya'll make her feel welcome as she comes to the stage to sing for all of you. He said come on up here Amber Newby.

Amber got up from her chair and walked toward the stage. She didn't seem at all nervous. She looked like a natural. She was so cute in her western outfit!

The colored lights from the dance floor and the lights from the stage made the sparkly dress glisten. She even got a few whistles from the crowd as she got up on the stage.

Amber put her hands around the microphone then I saw her lean over toward Jerry. She had told Jerry what song she could sing and the band kicked off with it. You guessed it! The number one song by Mystic. Play Crazy!

When Amber started singing, the crowd went wild. She had such a country twang to her voice as she sang! She had perfect timing and her pitch was right on. She wasn't a bit nervous! Or if she was, she didn't show it!

As she sang the words:

Play crazy on the radio,
So I won't be alone and blue,
Like Patsy Cline,
Back in time,
I was crazy for l o v i n g you..........

you'd thought it was Mystic herself up on the stage.

Amber sang another song. Some of the crowd was hollering "is that Mystic in the house"! Other's were hollering "Is that Mystic's kinfolks! I was even amazed! She was really that good!!! She did sound like Mystic!!

Even though I'd heard her sing along with the radio and sing around the house and at work, the live music really showed how talented she was!

Jerry came off the stage while the band played for Amber and we danced. We didn't get to do that very often. Most of the time, Jerry had to stay on the stage to get bad singers down after one song. Amber was holding her own! He let her continue on with the band.

Jerry was whispering in my ear as we danced. He had always been pretty good at figuring people. He'd been on the road and around so many. He said to me that Amber was a good singer but something in her eyes told him to be cautious.

I said, ah, she's okay. I like her. She is strange sometimes though! Then I said to Jerry, maybe she's just nervous, though in my mind I knew she didn't seem to be!

As I had my head on Jerry's shoulder while we danced, I was watching Amber as she was singing up on the stage. She was watching us. I thought I saw a little bit of jealousy in her eyes. I'd saw that look many times before.

It was then that I told Jerry that maybe Amber was a little jealous of us dancing. I told him that she didn't have a guy friend. She didn't have a date for the dance. Maybe that's what he'd saw in her eyes!

He said he thought I was wrong. He said he'd saw that same look in her eyes back when he had first met her over a month ago!

He said to me, please be careful Sandy! He didn't say anything else about Amber after that. I put all my thoughts away and held on tightly to Jerry as we danced.

Amber had sung two songs and was on her third one. The song was about to end so Jerry had to head back to the stage.

Once Jerry was back on the stage, he took his microphone in his hand. Jerry said to the crowd; I better watch out. I might lose my job here.

The crowd was still hollering. He said to the crowd of people, what do ya'll think of Amber! The crowd started screaming and whistling again!

As Amber got down from the stage, a lot of people were coming up to her and telling her how great she was! Most of them of course were males!

Jerry and his band kicked off a song. I listened to them play while I watched Amber as she was taking in all the attention from the hovering crowd.

Then after a while, after Amber had finally made her way to set down at our table and the crowd around her had returned to their seats, another young man came over to where we were all setting. He had asked Amber to dance. They danced and danced.

It didn't seem very long before it was time to go home. Most of the crowd had already left. The band was breaking down their equipment. Jerry was packing his guitar into its case while he and I were talking to each other.

He told me he'd come to my house as quick as he could get the band paid and everyone had left the building.

I told him I'd see him there and kissed him goodbye, then gathered our gang to leave. I had told him that I'd have to drop everyone off back at the salon and then head home myself.

My gang headed out of the dance hall and loaded into the van. As we were riding in the company van heading back to the salon, Amber couldn't quit talking about how much fun she had. Everyone else was quiet. I think most of them had fallen asleep.

I ask her about the man she had danced with? She said his name was Todd Adams. She said he wanted to see her again! Amber was so excited!

The drive back to the salon seemed so long. It was suddenly quiet. Even Amber had nodded off to sleep.

It was around 3am when we arrived. I woke everyone up and they hauled out of the company van and proceeded to their own cars. I went to my car and drove home and waited for Jerry's arrival.

I had fallen asleep on the couch. A knock on the door had awakened me. It was Jerry. He had brought the daylight with him. It was 6am.

I fixed us breakfast and then we both crashed together on the couch. Our time together was sweet but short. Jerry had to leave before lunch to do another show in another town.

I hated when he had to leave but that was his life. A life he loved! A life he had always wanted! Jerry and I said our goodbyes and until next time as I watched him leave my drive once again.

Amber and Todd did see each other again. They had only known each other for a few weeks. They were going out quiet a bit. She had been late for work a few times since they were dating. She hardly spent any time with us away from the salon, not that she did that much anyway.

Everything was Todd this or Todd that. She was even talking marriage. I tried to talk to her. I said "don't you think its a little soon to be talking marriage"?

She'd say that "her mother used to preach to her about her decisions of things and for me not to butt into her business".

I left things at that and hoped she'd make the right choice for herself. She was a grown woman!

It wasn't long that Amber started getting a way about her that I didn't understand nor like. It was more than just her being possessive of me. It was a deeper personality change. It was nothing like I'd ever saw before!

She was not socializing with any of us girls except when we were at work and sometimes she didn't socialize at work! She stayed at home all of the time, unless she and Todd were going out. Her mouth was getting vulgar and she was drinking booze. She was even making smart hurtful remarks about things that didn't even concern her.

When ever I would ask her what was wrong with her, she blamed it on her new bow Todd Adams. She claimed he was pressuring her to marry him.

I told her that she didn't have to take her problems out on others around her. I told her that she needed to tell Todd Adams where to get off!

She did apologize but it didn't stop her actions. Amber was a totally different person most times. Her mood changed as fast as daylight to dark! She had seemed to become somewhat evil like! How had Todd Adams caused such a change in her? What was he doing to her? Amber was becoming a hateful evil bitch!

CHAPTER 8

THE CAR ACCIDENT

One night after work, I was driving home. It was late November. There was a chill in the air. You could tell that winter time wasn't very far away!

The skies were dark from the rain clouds. The rain was beating against the windshield of my car. You could barely see your hand in front of your face it was so dark. The windshield wipers were on there highest speed as they slapped loudly against the windshield to clear the rain.

The windows were fogging up due to the rain and chill outside. I turned the defroster on high. The defroster wasn't clearing the windows very well which made it harder to see out.

I was about 20 miles from home on a dark narrow road that I'd traveled many times before. There weren't any kind of lights to light the roadway except for the headlights from my car.

There was no other form of human life for miles and no other vehicles on the road to home in sight. It was a scary darkness! An eerie feeling!

Then I saw the headlights of an oncoming car. The car's lights were on high beam. They were blinding my sight.

I lifted a hand to try to shield the light from my eyes! The car was approaching me very fast! I flashed my headlights to try to get the driver of that vehicle to dim their lights! No response!

I knew the approaching car was on my side of the road! I began hollering as if the other driver could hear me! You idiot, get on your side of the road! You are going to kill us both!

The car was headed straight into mine! I jerked my steering wheel to the right to try to miss the on coming car! That's the last thing I remember.

I woke up at the hospital. Things were blurry but I could see that I had a cast on my ankle. It was broken! My shoulder hurt! My head hurt!

When I awoke, I could vaguely make out the faces that were standing around my hospital bed when I heard someone say, do you know who we are?

I pointed and said, Jerry, the love of my life. He leaned down and kissed me. He said I'm glad you are alright. I missed you.

Then I saw my dearest friend in the whole world. Amelia! I hadn't seen her in a long time. That didn't matter.

This friend Amelia was the kind of friend that understood what friendship was about. The kind of friend that's always there when you need them and knows the other understood when you couldn't be around. We knew each others deepest secrets. Things only God knew about us. She just grabbed my hand and held it.

As I looked around the hospital room, I began calling out names. I said there is Amber and Todd, Carolyn, Pam, Patricia and Tammy. Then I ask where Meagan and Anita were. I knew they had to be here too!

Amelia was about to tell me where they were, then I saw them coming through the door. I said "there they are" I see them!

A doctor was following them in. The doctor checked me over and said looks like your going to be okay, except you won't be able to stand on that foot for a while.

He said I had a concussion. He said I'd been out for a couple of days. The doctor gave me my going home orders. He said that I would need someone with me to help me up and down until I was able to get around by myself, and again, he said; stay off the foot!

Amber quickly spoke up and said I live with her! I will take care of her! Sandy has been good to me, so this is the least I can do!

I thought to myself, now that's how a person is supposed to act. Then I thought about how Amber could take some "friend" lessons from my friend Amelia! But at least Amber was sounding like her old self. She was good when she wanted to be!

I was released from the hospital that day. Jerry and Amber drove me home in Jerry's car. Amber had came to the hospital with Jerry when they were called about the accident.

On the way home Jerry told me that Amber had never left my side since I had been brought into the hospital. He said Amber was worried about me.

Then Amber began telling me what had happened. She said the cops say that a passerby had spotted my car off the side of the road and stopped to help me. She said the passerby called 911 and had got help to me.

She said another car was headed toward mine and I must have turned the wheel to keep from being hit head on and that I had landed my car upside down in a ditch.

Amber asks me did I see or remember anything. I said no.

Then she went on to say that the driver of the other vehicle didn't stop to see if anyone was hurt. They left the scene.

She said that the cops had no way of knowing who the driver was of the other vehicle that had run me off the road.

Then Amber told me about how the cops said that there was only a smudge of car paint from the other vehicle that was transferred to my vehicle. They will probably never know who did this she said! Amber seemed so concerned. She appeared to be angry!

Soon we arrived at my house. Jerry helped me inside. He and Amber got me settled on the couch. Jerry stayed for a while but had to get back on the road. He was headed to California for a concert.

Jerry asks Amber if she was sure about staying and taking care of me. Once Amber reassured Jerry she'd be here for me, he said his goodbyes and told me he'd call me once he arrived in California.

Amber did take care of me. She waited on me hand and foot. Even Amber's bow Todd was nice enough to come during the evenings to check on me. That's what he told me anyway. That he came to see how I was doing. I really think he came to spend time with Amber.

With Amber's help and the other girls, and Amelia by my side as much as possible, and Jerry who checked on me daily by phone, and sent me candy and get well cards, I was making a nice recovery.

Time goes by. It was now nearing Christmas. It was less than a month away. What was I going to do about Christmas gifts for everyone! I wasn't going to be able to go out shopping for anything!

Then a thought came to me. During my time down I would knit some special gifts for everyone. My great granny

Tucker had taught me how to knit many years ago before she had died. I hoped I could still remember how!

Just the thought of making gifts for everyone made me feel better. It would also help me pass the recovering time.

I ask Amber to bring some yarn home after work one day. She did. I began to knit. It took a few tries but I finally remembered how! At least I would be using my time wisely, I thought. I couldn't do anything else.

Amber didn't care for Amelia. I learned that by watching as they cared for me. Amber had even remarked that "if Amelia was the friend I thought she was, she'd be here for me 24/7". A friend never should leave you she had said!

I tried to make Amber understand! Amelia and I had been friends for over 20 years! We both know that we have our own lives to live! We know that when we needed the other we would always be there whenever we could be! That's what a real friend was about, I told her! Amber just didn't understand.

A couple weeks had passed. Finally I was back on my feet. I was back at work. It was a week until Christmas. Thank goodness I had all my gifts ready for everyone. It would be a busy week at the salon and there was no time to be out shopping!

The pressure of work and getting ready for the holidays were building. Everybody was wanted their hair permed and or wanting their nails done before the Christmas holidays.

We were planning a big Christmas party for all of us who worked in the salon! Jerry's band would play for us at the Continental Club. We would have our dinner catered by one of the finest caterers. We would exchange gifts. It would be a fun and happy time once we worked out the final plans for it.

All during this time, the one thing that made things worse was that Amber was being her distant bitchy hateful evil self again. You could tell that she didn't really want anything to do with planning a Christmas party.

That put a strain on everybody. Everyone else was taking part in making the party happen and finally it did happen! The Christmas party was a success except that Amber didn't even show up!

Everyone had even brought gifts to the party for Amber. Ambers no show kind of put a damper on everything. She had caused everyone to be somewhat depressed though everybody tried to have a good time.

After the party was over, all of Amber's gifts were loaded into the trunk of my car. I took them home and placed them into her bedroom. Amber wasn't at home when I got there. I figured she must be out with Todd.

I changed into my pajamas and headed to my bedroom. I had just gotten myself comfortable in my bed when my cell phone started ringing. I answered the phone and on the other end was Jerry. We talked for more than an hour. I had gotten so sleepy while talking on the phone that I fell asleep with the phone to my ear. The last words I recall that Jerry had said to me were that he loved me.

The morning came early. Amber hadn't come home the whole night. Christmas was over.

CHAPTER 9

AMBER GETS AN ATTITUDE

The salon was opened back up for business the day after Christmas. It was slow. The day seemed to drag by. Amber had gotten a few complaints from some of the clients. It wasn't so much about the manicures as it was about her attitude. She had insulted some of them. She had made some awful remarks about them.

It was going to be a new year soon. Matter of fact, the New Year was just a week away. I really needed to call Amber into the conference room. We needed to set some things straight before things got out of hand!

I went to her and told her that we needed to talk. She said to me, what ever, in a smart like way!

I looked at her and said that I wouldn't take that tone from her. I was mad! I told her that I wanted her to go to the conference room now!

Like a child, she just jerked her body around and headed toward the conference room. I followed her.

She stood just inside the door as I went in past her. I turned around to look at her after I entered the room. She had this glaring look in her eyes!

I told her to take a seat. I said to her, this may take a while. She went on into the room and set down. I could tell that she didn't want to. I took a seat at the table facing Amber.

I begin to tell her about the complaints I had gotten on her. I told her that they needed to stop. I demanded that they stop! Amber just rolled her eyes and looked around the room!

I ask Amber what was causing her to treat people the way she was treating them. She just looked at me! It was a look of someone who might be mad and crazy at the same time!

She said she wasn't and hadn't done what she was being accused of! She didn't seem to want to hear what I was saying to her.

I was getting irate! I was even raising my voice at Amber! I had never in my whole life been this upset or aggravated at anyone like this before.

I guess after a while Amber saw that I wasn't going to tolerate any negative things happening in the salon and she finally apologized.

She never admitted to any wrong doing but said if she had done anything that she was sorry. Then she said it wouldn't happen again!

Finally my temper calmed! I told Amber that we would be closing the salon for the holidays. Maybe a few days away from the salon would do us all some good. I told her we would start with a fresh outlook when we returned after the New Year! Finally finished with our talk, I told Amber she could get back to work.

After Amber had left the conference room, I continued to set in there for a while. I lit a cigarette and puffed on it.

As usual, the way that my mind worked overtime, I begin thinking about Amber and the things that had been going on since she began working for me. She was such a strange individual. You couldn't help but love her but you could hate her when she was acting up. I had never met anyone like her before.

One thing I knew for sure was if Amber continued to harm my salon by her attitude with the clients I would have to make some changes. I hoped I wouldn't have to do that!

I looked at the clock on the wall in the conference room. I would have an appointment coming in any time. I put out the cigarette. I got up and went back into the salon at my work area.

The day didn't pass by fast enough for me! I was still angry with Amber though I tried not to let it show to anyone! I guess I hid it pretty well. Nobody seemed to notice! No one questioned me! Finally the day ended. We closed the salon and I went home.

By the time I arrived at home Amber was already there. I could see her sitting at the kitchen table when I entered the house from the living room. I didn't know if she was eating or just setting there.

I went to my bedroom. I didn't want to speak to her unless I just had to. I surely didn't want to bring up anything about work. I believed that work and any problems of work should be left at work.

Although I did keep my eye on Amber through out the evening when ever she would walk past my bedroom door! She had passed my bedroom at least four or five times within a couple of hours. Why I don't know! She had never had that much energy! Maybe she was walking off her stress!

Other than pacing the floor; she seemed to act as if nothing had happened or had been said to her. Plus, she never spoke a word to me either! Maybe, like me, she was leaving work at work! That was good I thought!

I was getting hungry for supper. I left from my bedroom and headed to the kitchen to find something to eat. I grabbed some leftovers from the fridge and warmed them.

I saw that Amber had put on a pot of coffee. I poured me a cup. I set down at the kitchen table and ate my supper. I cleaned my mess I'd made and then went back to my bedroom.

I turned on the radio to listen to some music while I straightened my bedroom. I had left it in such a mess while getting ready for work that morning. Finally with my room picked up, I headed to the bathroom to shower. I washed my hair and my body then stepped out and towel dried myself off. I wrapped my hair in a towel then stood at the mirror and put on my night moisturizer. I then blow dried my hair.

It was now bedtime. I was so tired! Heading back to my bedroom, I got ready for bed. I fell asleep as quickly as my head had hit the pillow.

The next morning came fast. I felt like I had slept on a rock! My head hurt! I grabbed an aspirin from my bedside table and popped it into my mouth hoping to ease my pain.

With a throbbing headache, I got up out of bed and did my usual routine of getting ready for work, did breakfast and then I made the long drive to work.

The day at work went fair. I didn't hear of any complaints of Amber. There was tension in the air though! I think all of the employees felt it. Thankful my headache had left me! I could hardly wait for the day to end!

Finally it was closing time! The next day at the salon was better and the next better than that! Amber was once again back to being her "good self"!!!

CHAPTER 10

A NEW YEAR

Soon it was December 31. We closed the salon that evening. It was on a Thursday. We would have a three day holiday. Friday, Saturday and Sunday! Maybe after a few days off and bringing in the New Year, even better days would follow.

Jerry had called me at work earlier in the day to see if I wanted to make plans to bring in the New Year with him. I told him that I'd love to, but that I didn't want to do anything special. I just wanted to be with him.

We decided that he and I would celebrate the New Year together at his home. I would go to his home over in Trina Alabama. I felt it would do me good to get away from my home for awhile.

Amber could have my house all by herself for the holidays. She and Todd had been fussing. I guessed she would spend her New Year all alone.

I had left the salon after work and drove straight to Alabama. When I arrived at Jerry's home he opened his front door for me to enter and in his hands were a dozen red roses. He handed them to me as he leaned toward me and wrapped his arms around me. He kissed me.

He was such a charmer! He pulled me tighter into his arms and then led me into his home.

Jerry's home was definitely that of a bachelor. He had his western clothing strewn all over the place along with his cowboy boots and hats. His kitchen sink was filled with dirty dishes. His refrigerator was practically bare. He was a typical male.

Jerry and I cuddled on the sofa for a while and talked. Then he and I had a candle light supper in his living room. He had made it all by himself. So he said! He had cooked rib eye steaks with baked potato's and salad! What he didn't know was that I saw the steak and salad boxes from the restaurant!

He didn't hide them very well! He had tried to push them to the bottom of the trash can but after washing my hands and throwing away a paper towel I saw the boxes! It didn't matter! It was delicious! All in all, I guess he did put the meal together by himself.

After we finished eating we went outside to sit on his back patio. His neighbors were doing the fire works thing. We sat and watched fire works as they were being blasted up towards the sky. It was a beautiful picture! We watched the glistening skies for about an hour. It was dark out. The night bugs were beginning to bite so we headed back inside his home.

Once again we snuggled together on his sofa and talked and laughed. He was so much fun to be with!

At the stroke of midnight Jerry and I were in each others arm. We had celebrated the last four New Years together and we didn't want to change anything now. I stayed overnight and woke up in his arms the next morning.

The morning had come too soon. Jerry had to get up and head back on the road. He had a show to do in Colorado. He would be gone for a week. He got ready to leave. Soon he had everything packed and we shared breakfast and he was out the door.

I hung around Jerry's home for most of the day. I cleaned up his place before I headed back to my house later that night.

When I arrived at my home that Friday night on the first of January, I heard someone in the kitchen. I walked into the kitchen. Amber was washing dishes. She had cleaned the house from top to bottom.

I remarked to her of how nice things looked and how clean the house smelled. She said she didn't have anything else to do and she didn't mind doing the things she had done.

I thanked her. Amber's good personality was coming out. Why couldn't she be like this all the time, I thought! I know everyone has a bad day every now and then, but pleeease!

A while later I was in the living room watching TV. I saw Amber out of the corner of my eye. She came to the couch and set down. She had brought in a glass of iced tea and handed it to me. I thanked her.

She and I began talking. It was like old times. It was actually fun. She begins to tell me about an incident she had seen happen at a store. She said a lady had went to reach for something off a top shelf. The lady was short she said. She said, and then this man came over to help the lady. The man reached for what the lady wanted. The man knocked everything off of the top shelf and the things came tumbling down right on top of the lady's head!

Amber had me laughing so hard I could barely catch my breath. The remainder of the night passed by quickly. I went to bed feeling better about Amber and her attitude. Saturday and Sunday passed.

The next day, Monday, January, 4th, at work and the days to follow were finally back to normal. Amber wasn't getting any more complaints. She was doing great work and treating the clients with respect. She was treating everyone with love and respect! When she was like this you couldn't help but love her!

It was late in the evening on a Saturday. Jerry wouldn't return from Colorado until later on in the night or what I call the wee hours of the morning.

I didn't feel like going anywhere. I thought maybe I was catching a cold or the flu. My feet hurt! I had stood on them all day at work. I just felt like setting at home.

I went to my bedroom and grabbed a blanket and a pillow. I then went to the living room and turned on the TV. I had just gotten snuggled up on the couch with my blanket when I realize Amber was at home.

I thought she had gone out for the night. But Todd had brought her home after they had been out for supper. She had come into the living room right after I had gotten comfortable on the couch.

Amber sat on the edge of the couch where I was lying. Amber and I began to talk. I ask her where Todd was. Amber started complaining about Todd. That didn't surprise me!

She began to tell me that Todd was going to hang out with a couple of his old friends that he hadn't seen in a long while. She said she and Todd had gotten into a fuss fight.

While we were talking, she asks would I mind if she hung out here with me. I wasn't surprised she wanted to hang around here. As usual, she didn't go anywhere unless she was with Todd. She always stayed at the house when they were fussing.

I told her it would be fine. I told her we'd watch a movie if she wanted to. Amber liked that idea. She stated that a movie was just what she needed. We chatted for a bit while waiting on the movie to start. The movie came on.

During the movie I got hungry. I ask Amber did she want a snack or something. She said sure. We both headed to the kitchen. She grabbed some peanuts and a bag of chips. I went to the refrigerator and got us a couple of sodas out.

Amber had already headed back to the TV. I decided that I wanted some peanut butter and crackers. I got the peanut butter out of the cabinet. I couldn't seem to find the crackers. I had always put them in the same place. I knew I should have crackers. I had just bought a new box.

After looking for a few minutes, I found them. They had gotten pushed all the way to the back of the cabinet. I guessed that Amber must have pushed them back. Maybe she hated crackers so much that she couldn't even stand the sight of the box.

I didn't dare to ask her about it. I didn't want to bring up any old feelings for her. Her mood had been that of good character. I didn't want to mess with that!

I made myself a stack of peanut butter and crackers. I put them on a small plate. I then reached into the cabinet and grabbed a bag of white powdered sugar coated donuts. They were my favorite snack!

I then headed back to the TV with the snacks and drinks. The movie we were watching was a scary flick from the 70's. I was so into the movie, I didn't realize I had eaten nearly the whole bag of chips that Amber had brought into the living room, and a half bag of donuts. I was full.

I ask Amber if she wanted the peanut butter crackers I had made. I told her I couldn't eat another bite. As quick as the words came out of my mouth I thought how stupid can you be Sandy! You know she hates crackers!

The look that Amber gave me, I couldn't explain. It gave me the shivers! I thought I saw a bit of anger in her eyes. For a moment she didn't say a word. I didn't either! Then she finally said no thanks with a calmer look. She said she was full.

I noticed she had only eaten maybe a handful of peanuts and had only had a sip or two of her soda. How could she be full I wondered! Though I was curious, I still didn't say another word! The room got quiet except for the TV.

My eyes and my mind were distracted from the movie that was on TV for I started thinking about the incident at the salon when Amber had thrown out the crackers.

I remembered her remark about not liking crackers that day at the grocery store. Why didn't she just say that she didn't like crackers this time, instead of saying she was full. I didn't dare question her about it. As before, I figured it was something in her past that she just didn't want to talk about.

It wasn't long before the movie was over, so I told Amber I was going to get ready for bed. She said she was too.

I grabbed up the blanket and pillow and went to my bedroom. I went to sleep thinking about Amber and what might have happen to her in her past to make her like she is. It must have been pretty bad, I thought.

CHAPTER 11

AMBER'S HOUSE

Another month had passed. It was already a week into February. Winter had set in. It was cold and snow had fallen to the ground. The weather forecast was predicting this to be the biggest snow and coldest day we'd had in over twenty years.

I hated the winter months. It was days like this that I dreaded getting out of bed. I wished that I could be like bears and hibernate and let the cold weather pass me by.

Knowing I couldn't hibernate, I managed to make myself get out of bed and get ready for work. On the drive to work, the snow was coming down heavy. I was glad that it was a dry snow!

The roads weren't too bad to drive on and they had gotten better by the time I had gotten closer to the city. The city officials had salted most of the roads to make the roads passable. I safely made it to work. All my employees had made it to work!

Business was slow due to the bad weather. It amazed me though to see anyone who would get out in the cold and snow for a hair do! It was always those little old ladies that couldn't miss getting their hair done! This particular morning was no different.

I watched out the salon window as a car slid up to the curb in front of the salon. A gentleman got out the drivers side of the car and came to the passenger side and opened the car door. I watched as he helped this little old lady out and he walked her up to the salon entrance.

As he opened the salon door for her to enter, I heard her say to him, now sonny you be back here at 10 o'clock. He promised her he'd be back! You could tell who the boss was of that mother and son relationship!

I knew that this day was going to be one of those days that we had plenty of free time on our hands. Sometime during the day while at the salon, Tammy had reminded me that Amber's birthday was coming up in a few weeks.

How could I have forgotten? After all, my birthday was the same day as hers. February 25th. I couldn't believe how the time had gone by. Amber had been working at the salon for a little over ten months now. This would be Ambers first birthday with us!

All through the morning I wondered about what kind of gift I could get for Ambers' birthday. I didn't know what she needed. She had never asks for anything or even hinted about anything she wanted.

After careful thought I had made my decision. Amber needed a home. A place to call her own! I would give her 1/2 acre of my land along with the little old cabin house that sat on it.

When my mother had passed away, she had left me everything she had. I had 50 acres of land. Most of it was wooded. The old cabin house was the one I had grown up in as a child. My daddy had built it long before he was killed in the coal mines.

The old place needed a little fixing up, but with some hard work I could have it ready for Amber by the time her birthday arrived.

My mother had lived there in the old home up until she died. Mother would be glad to know that someone would be living in our old house. I didn't have any use for the old place.

A few years before my mother passed away, she had helped me out financially to get my own house built that I live in now.

I had begged my mother to move in it with me, but she refused! She loved the old cabin home! She didn't need to have all that city stuff she'd say! Before I had decided to build on the property, I had told my mother that I needed to be closer to the city since I had my business and all there!

My mother had pitched a fit about that plan! She needed and wanted me close to her! She wouldn't here me! When my mothers mind was made up, you didn't argue with her! I ended up doing as she wanted me to do and staying close to her.

I had my house built to set a bit closer to the front of the property line. The old cabin home was set way back into the woods a good distance away from mine. My house was built with an up to date design. It consists of features with all the conveniences of the city with a country setting.

It was nothing at all like the old house. The old place had an out house that stood way in the back. As a child, I hated having to go to the bathroom. It was always scary and especially at night. The water we drank came from a well. That I sometimes miss.

My mother did eventually have an indoor toilet put inside the old house just before she died but the water was still pumped out from the old well though. The old out house had pretty much caved into the ground. It was now closed off. It had been filled with soil to keep animals from falling into it.

The old house was heated with wood from a fireplace. If the fireplace was still in working order, there would be enough timber on the property for Amber to cut up for her fire wood. You could barely see the old home place now. It was all grown up with tall trees and weeds.

I figured that giving the old house to Amber would give her privacy. She needed it now that she had Todd coming around and calling on her. Even though Todd and Amber fussed a lot, Todd always kept coming back to Amber. Amber always took him back.

In a way, I guessed maybe Amber's anger in the past was because we had been getting on each others nerves. Even though I loved Amber, she was beginning to get on my nerves!

It has always been said that two families can't live in the same household. It seems that we have proven that to be true! Being away from each other would do us both good!

I told the girls at the salon about what I wanted to give Amber for her birthday. They had all decided that they wanted to pitch in with there time and money and help with fixing the place up. This would be their birthday gift to her from them. After all, they had come to love Amber just like I had.

Amber somehow made you care about her very deeply. Even when she was being her bitchy self, you felt sorry for her! Besides, aren't we all a little bitchy sometimes I thought to myself!

With plans in place, the first thing was to make everything legal. By the late afternoon, the snow that had fallen had melted. The weather forecasters had predicted wrong. Even though it was very cold outside, the sun had came out and had cleared the snow away.

I decided that after work I'd go to my lawyer's office and get the papers drawn up. The work day ended. I went to the lawyer's office and told him what I wanted to have done. My lawyer thought it was strange and unusual for me to want to just give property away and he was totally against me doing so!

I went against his judgment. That's what I wanted to do! I told him I wanted it done quickly and wanted it so that all I had to do was have Amber sign the papers and then give the deed to Amber.

Though my lawyer was against it, it didn't take him very long to get the legal paper work drawn up. Now Amber could have the house and half acre for her birthday. But first we must get to the repairs and such on the place!

After work and while I was at home, my phone was ringing off the hook. Amber had arrived home too and was in her bedroom. Every time that my phone would ring, Amber would come around to where ever I might be at the time and she saw me on my phone. I could tell that Amber knew something was up, but she never questioned anything.

The girls were calling my phone whenever they thought of something they had for the old house. All of us talked about the things we could do to fix up the old place. We discussed about our biggest concern which would be finding a way to sneak back to the old place without Amber seeing any of us. We had to be cautious.

In the meantime, I called and told Jerry about giving Amber the place and what our plans were. He didn't think it was such a good idea, but I, like my mother, was stubborn and had made up my mind!

Jerry said he could help us out by cutting a trail in from behind the old house before he left for his next show. He told me that he'd borrow his neighbor farmer's lawn tractor and make a path for us to travel. He said we would be able to enter from the back of the property without Amber seeing what was going on.

That will helped out so much I told him. Jerry said he would be gone on the road for only a couple of days this time. He was going to do an over night show in Georgia. He said he'd come back to help out again when he returned.

The girls and I had discussed what and how we'd do things to get started. We all would bring furniture and things from our homes that we didn't need or use anymore. We'd fix the house up really nice for Amber!

The next day, late in the evening, Amber had left with Todd. I called Jerry. He contacted the farmer about the lawn tractor. He went over and borrowed it and brought the tractor to the old home place and cut the trail he had promised to cut.

The girls and myself gathered together and began working on the old house. We loaded a pick up truck with furniture and other things we had collected from our homes. Everything seemed to be coming together!

As the days passed by it got easier to get to the old house. We didn't have to worry so much about Amber either! As most of the time, Amber was usually with Todd. Some nights she didn't even come home. She was staying many of the nights over at Todd's place.

Mostly all of our free time was spent working to get the house ready. Thankful, Jerry had been to Georgia and had now come back.

Jerry was a jack of all trades. He did all of the plumbing repairs to the old house. He cleared the land of all the over grown weeds. He mended the broken fence and patched a few holes in the walls. He repaired the stair rails that wobbled. He checked the well water that ran up to the old house. It was all good.

The whole time that we worked on the place we didn't dare tell Todd, for fear he might give the secret away. We wanted to surprise Amber in a big way.

While getting the place ready for Amber all of us had decided that we would give Amber her birthday gift to her on the Saturday night at the next girls sleep over which would be in as little as two weeks. It would be just a day before her birthday.

The days were going by fast. We were hanging wall papering, painting, repairing, cleaning and decorating the house. We weren't even sure that we'd finish the house in time!

We were down to one more week to complete the house. By this time, Jerry had left to go back on his tours. He'd be gone on two road tours this time. He promised he'd call me between the gigs. He had been a huge help but there was still plenty left for us to do!

Day to day, everyone was coming after work to complete the house for Amber. It was like we would get two steps forward and then go three steps back.

Finally we did get finished. It was a Friday night late on the twenty third. The next day, Saturday, February 24th, at work, we all were so tired but somehow we were making it okay.

Amber questioned us as to why we were all tired looking. She stated that what few times she had seen any of us lately that we had seemed worn out. Amber had even remarked about how we all looked hung over! She knew that none of us drank. She just didn't know!

This would be the night that we would give Amber her birthday present. While at work, I reminded Amber of our sleep over. She thanked me for reminding her and said she would see us there. Amber then told me that she would be late getting there. She said that Todd was taking her out to supper right after work.

I thought this couldn't have worked out any better! Amber being with Todd would give us extra time to get the things ready for her birthday party at my house. Thank goodness that Amber and Todd weren't fussing!

CHAPTER 12

THE BIRTHDAY PARTY

Finally it was 6pm. It was time to close up shop. After closing the salon all of us left for home. Everyone had arrived at my house to get things ready for the birthday party with the exception of Amber. It was around 7:30pm when all had arrived.

Each one was designated a project. Carolyn was chosen to keep a watch out for Amber and let us know when Amber was arriving. Someone would hang balloons and streamers around the living room while the others set the table with the cake and ice cream and napkins and such.

A short time passed. Finally everything was ready! We heard Carolyn holler. Here she comes. We all hid about the living room!

It seemed like Amber was never going to make it to the door. Then finally we heard Amber unlocking the door to my house. When Amber walked in everyone hollered SURPRISE!!!! Amber realized it was not just a sleep over. It was a birthday party for her.

We could hardly wait to give Amber her birthday gift. Everybody was excited! After hugs were exchanged all of us got settled around the living room.

I begin to speak! I told Amber that she was appreciated so much for everything she had done for me at the salon. We all really loved her, we told her! I laughed and said except when you are being bitchy! Everyone laughed! They knew what I was talking about! I laughed as I told Amber that I thought she'd been around Tammy to long!

Amber didn't have any comment. I then proceeded to tell her that the gift she was about to receive was from the whole gang. We hope you get lots of use of it, I said.

I handed her an envelope. Amber looked at it. On the front it read Amber's Deed to her house and land. Amber was speechless. She just stared at the envelope in her hand. She didn't show any kind of emotion! She didn't even attempt to open it.

Then we begin to tell her about the house and the work we had done and how hard it was to keep it a secret. We were all excited!

Anxious, I told Amber to open the envelope. All of us were coaxing her to open it! She finally opened it. I told her that my lawyer said for her to sign on this line. I pointed to the line on the deed. I handed her an ink pen. She signed, and then I signed below her.

It was final. The place was Amber's. I went to my copier and made a copy for my lawyer and then I handed the deed back to Amber.

With excitement for Amber, we all decided to go over to the old cabin house and show Amber her new home. As soon as Amber walked into the old house she couldn't believe how beautiful it looked. She cried and cried. This was the first and only time I'd ever seen Amber cry!

Amber stated that she didn't even know that a house had existed there. How did ya'll do this, she said? She was excited! That good part of Amber that you loved was showing thru. She was so thankful. All she could say was "thank you so much" over and over! It was at that very moment, that I was glad that I had decided to give the place to Amber.

After showing off the place we loaded up and headed back to my house. When we arrived back at my house, we all headed inside and then I got a big "SURPRISE" myself.

Tammy had stayed behind without me knowing, and had set up for my birthday too. Everyone was hollering Happy Birthday! Surprise!

Amber had known about the party they were giving me she had said. Looks like they got both of us! Amber and I laughed! We all got a good laugh about that! It was nice to see Amber smile and actually really laugh and include herself with the rest of us!

We all had cake and ice cream and we talked to each other about Amber's new place she would be moving into. We were having loads of fun!

A while later Amber and Tammy stood up in front of everyone. To my surprise, they presented me with a round trip airfare ticket to Las Vegas. They said I needed a vacation. They said after all I'd been thru lately, getting over the car accident, it would do me good to get away for a few days.

Everyone said Amber had come up with the idea of a vacation gift for me. They had all agreed with her that it was the best gift and everyone had pitched in and bought the ticket.

They also gave me a debit card with $500 dollars on it to spend while I would be in Vegas. They said maybe I'd hit big money at the casino's and we all could just retire! I was totally shocked and thankful!

We were all having a great time celebrating both Amber and my birthday. Everyone was sitting around in my living room talking and laughing! I was looking at the airline ticket and saw that the date was for Sunday, February 25th, my birthday.

I began to say to everyone, hey, this ticket is for tomorrow!! I'd be hopping on an airplane in the morning headed to Las Vegas.

They began to tell me that that was why they had given the ticket to me now instead of waiting to give it to me on my birthday tomorrow. It was the only flight they could get!

I was panicking! I don't have time to pack! I told them! I don't have anyone to take care of "FANCY HAIR & MANICURES'; and I won't be getting back until Wednesday! What was I going to do?!!

They all assured me that things would be taken care of and for me not to worry. They would care for the salon.

Quickly, Amber then went and grabbed a suitcase and said let's get her packed. We all went running around like crazy people trying to get things packed for me to leave the next morning. My suitcase was now filled and setting by the front door.

Carolyn had made the suggestion that we should all call it a night and everyone go home since I would have to leave early to get to the airport in the morning. Everyone had agreed with her.

It was nearly 9:30pm.Our gathering had been short but sweet! Everyone hugged me as they were getting ready to leave and wished me a safe trip and assured me again everything would be fine. They all wished me a happy birthday for Sunday since they wouldn't see me. I'd be in Vegas!

Everyone had also wished Amber a happy birthday too. They wouldn't see her until Monday. She had said to all of us that Todd was taking her out of town to celebrate her birthday.

While everyone was getting ready to leave, I told Amber that the electricity wouldn't be turned on until Monday at the house I had given her, so she would have stay with me for the night unless she was going to go stay with Todd until then.

She was okay with staying at my house for the night. She said Todd was picking her up Sunday for her birthday. Again she told me that he was taking her out of town to celebrate!

Amber then told me that she would be moved out of my home by the time I got back from Vegas. I said there was no hurry but what ever she wanted to do would be fine.

While Amber and I were standing at my front door as everyone was leaving, I jokingly, told them that I was turning off my cell phone and not turning it back on until I returned from Vegas!

Amber and I waved goodbye to everyone as they got into their cars and was driving away. Amber then left the living room and went to her bedroom to go to sleep. I went to my bedroom. I didn't know it then, but the remark I had made about turning off my cell phone was a huge big mistake!

CHAPTER 13

RESTLESS FOR VEGAS!

With everyone gone home and Amber had gone to bed, I went to bed too. I looked at the clock as I lay in bed. It was 10:30pm. Then it was 11pm. I just couldn't sleep. I guessed it was due to the anticipation of having to get up early for a trip to Vegas on an airplane, I thought!

I wasn't hungry but I decided that I'd go to the kitchen and have a snack and a glass of milk. Maybe that would help me rest.

As I was going down the hall towards the kitchen I felt like someone was watching me. I thought I'd heard a strange noise! I could feel the sense that something wasn't right. God seemed to have a way of letting me know when things weren't quiet right. Even though sometimes I didn't listen! That inner voice was telling me something was very wrong!

Being a little frightened, I called out to Amber. She didn't answer. I guessed she was asleep.

My heart started pounding. I could hear it beating in my head! I felt like my heart was going to come right out of my chest. Amber! I called her again. Nearly screaming her name! Still she didn't answer.

Even though I had this eerie feeling, I went on into the kitchen. I looked all around. I didn't see anyone. Maybe it was just my imagination, I thought! Then the eerie feelings began to subside. My heart beat slowed back down to normal. I thought again that it was just my imagination!

I got the milk out of the refrigerator and went to the cabinet to reach for a glass. I had just gotten the glass into my hand! All of a sudden the milk and the glass fell out of my hands as I felt something stabbing me in my back! Could it be a gun? Was it a knife?

My heart started racing again! Then I tried to turn around and see who? What? I thought I'd saw something shiny!

Then I felt a burning in my eyes. I had been sprayed with mace. I couldn't see anything! I screamed!

I screamed to Amber for help! I screamed to God for help! I was screaming to whoever it was that had just mace me! Who are you, I yelled? What do you want? I didn't hear a sound!

I then felt my wrist being tied together. I began kicking at who ever this was attacking me! Screaming to turn me loose!

Even though I couldn't see from being maced, my eyes were being blind folded! Why would someone be covering my eyes? I couldn't see nothing!

All I felt and smelled was the liquored breath of the person that was doing this to me and their cold clammy hands that had tied my wrist together!

I was being dragged across the floor like a rag doll. I was still kicking and trying to get loose! Where are you taking me, I screamed? Still no answer!

I screamed for Amber again to help me! Had someone hurt Amber? Why are you doing this to me, I said? Still no answer! "Who are you" I kept screaming to the attacker! Then I felt something hit me in the back of my head.

I must have passed out or I had been knocked out cold! When I came to myself, I was tied up in a straight chair that was in my bedroom.

My feet, legs and hands were strapped to the chair. My eyes had been uncovered. I looked around the room. Nothing looked out of place. Nobody was around.

I would scream, but I had been gagged with tape around my mouth. Who would hear me anyway? I was miles and miles away from anyone.

Where was Amber, I wondered? If I could get to my cell phone, but my hands were tied. I didn't see my cell phone anywhere anyhow! Someone must have taken it! I'd always left it on my bedside table at night! It wasn't there!

Then I heard a noise coming from another part of the house! It was getting closer! Who is this, I thought? Again I felt my heart pounding intensely! I thought I was going to have a heart attack! What did they want! Where was Amber? God help me!

I was watching the door from my bedroom as the noise was getting closer. It sounded like keys rattling. Then I saw the person! It was Amber!

I was trying to tell her by motion to get me loose; that someone had came in the middle of the night and had tied me up. Maybe we were robbed I thought!

Then I realized that Amber wasn't helping me! Why wasn't she helping me? My head was hurting. I felt like I'd been hit with a hammer.

Amber came closer to me. She reached and jerked the tape from my mouth. The way she yanked the tape, I knew that she was the one that had did this to me. Why? Was this Amber's way of making a sick joke? If so, it sure wasn't funny!

Why Amber, I ask her? What have I done to you? She didn't say a word. She then turned and went back out of the room.

I could hear her shuffling around from the outside of my bedroom door. I hollered out, Amber, what are you doing? She came back to the door of my bedroom. The look I saw in her green eyes looked like the devil.

She said "you can scream, but nobody will hear you! She said I've lived here with you long enough to know that!

Amber then walked over to me and I noticed she had her work bag in her hand. She set on the edge of the bed facing me. She opened her work bag that she had laid onto her lap.

I watched as she took out her nail file. She held it like a knife and started making like she was cutting her hands, then her throat and moved it up toward her face toward her eyes.

She then looked at me and said I think you need a good manicure. Then she started moving the file towards me. I was screaming! God! God, please help me! My heart was pounding again! My heart was going to burst right out of my chest!

She mimicked the same movements with the file that she had done on herself on my hands, throat and face.

I was terrified. I could barely speak, but managed to get the words "Amber, let me help you" out of my mouth.

She just started laughing!!! Then she said, screaming and angrily at me, I don't need your f---ing help, I don't need anyone's help!!! You are the one that needs help she yelled at me!!!

I was trying to break free from the ropes that had me tied to the chair! I did need help! I had no idea of how I was going to get out of this situation.

I got quiet as I kept a watchful eye on Amber and of what she might do to me next. In my mind, I prayed to God. Please God, Help me thru these things I am about to come upon, put your hand in mine and don't let go. Help me get out of this alive. Be with me.

I had never been real close to God, at least not like God wanted me to be, but I did know him. Would he see me through? Is he really there when you need him most? I prayed. He had always seen me thru things before. Then I thought about my great granny Tucker and what she had taught me about prayer. He would be with me!

I watched as Amber reached around at the back of the chair I was tied in. She was untying the ropes that were wrapped around my waist holding me in the chair. Amber then pulled me up from the chair. My hands, legs and feet still tied together.

Amber led me outside into my yard. I was trying to take baby steps to keep from falling. I was stumbling. Amber was shoving me. I fell down on my face. I felt the asphalt dig into my face. I couldn't get up. She was dragging me.

She put me in her car. I could see that it was just becoming daylight out. It must be Sunday morning, I thought. I should be heading to the airport. It was my birthday! It was Amber's birthday.

Where are you taking me; I screamed at her! She said, you'll see. She was so hateful sounding.

Amber took me to the cabin house that we all had worked so hard on for her. I was thinking to myself, why in the world is she taking me there?

When Amber got me inside the old house she dragged me up the stairs. Her arms were locked under mine from behind as she pulled me! I was still trying to get away. I wasn't going to make it easy for her!

Soon she had reached her destination. She shoved me into a large closet of one of the rooms in the house. It was in the very room that I had spent most of my childhood. I had played with my dolls in this room. I learned to style hair in this room!

With my hands, my legs and my feet still tied up, I couldn't get away, even though I tried! Amber had attached a chain to the closet walls. She had tied me to the chains. She also put tape back over my mouth.

She said to me, nobody can hear you, but that she was tired of hearing me yell. She then closed me up in the closet. I was in total darkness.

I could hear Amber as she was going down the stairs. I wondered what she was going to do. I then heard a door slam. Had Amber left? I prayed that she had!

I kept trying to get myself loose. I kept trying to scream, but Amber was right. Nobody would ever hear me, even if my mouth hadn't been gagged.

CHAPTER 14

HAPPY BIRTHDAY TO ME

A little later, what seemed like hours, I heard someone? I could hear them coming up the stairs. It was Amber! She was humming a song.

She opened the closet door and just stared in at me. She was leaning up against the door frame of the closet.

Her expression was like something I'd never seen before. It was a devilish death look in her eyes!

She said, Okay bitch, I'm back! Sorry I had to leave you, no I'm not, but I had to go back and clean up your filthy place.

Amber then said that she didn't want anyone to get suspicious if they happened to drop by my house. She said she had left a mess over there. Not that anyone was going to be coming by she'd said! Then she reminded me that everyone thought I was in Vegas!

Then Amber said Oh yeah! By the way, happy birthday! She then started singing HAPPY BIRTHDAY TO YOU, HAPPY BIRTHDAY TO YOU, HAPPY BIRTHDAY DEAR SANDY HAPPY BIRTHDAY TO YOU!!!!!

I was right! It was Sunday!! My birthday! It wasn't a very happy birthday though. Had Amber totally lost her mind?

I knew she was strange at times, but she was nothing like I'd ever saw her before! Was she drunk or high on drugs! What was going on?

I then watched Amber as she sat down on the floor in the doorway of the closet. She started talking. She started crying. She said sounding almost sympathetic; Sandy, I'm sorry that I have to do this to you, but sometimes you just don't have any control on the way things are.

I could tell from the slur of her words that Amber was slightly intoxicated. She kept talking!

She said I hoped things would be different, but things never change. She began telling me that I had treated her badly, just like the way her mother used to treat her. What did she mean by all this?!

Then she said to me; you chose your friends over me, when I thought I was your best friend. She said you left me alone at home when you should have stayed with me. You never liked the way I looked. You tried to change the way I dressed, the way I wore my hair.

While Amber was saying all these things, I then noticed that Amber was dressed like she was when I first saw her. She had on a t-shirt with her boy cut jeans and sneakers. Her hair was straight and falling in her face. She was sporting her tomboy look.

Amber continued to talk. She said I saw the way you looked at me when I was on the stage that night with Jerry's band. I know you two were talking about me! I could never please you.

I tried to tell Amber that she was wrong about everything she was saying, but I still had my mouth covered with the gag. She wasn't listening anyway. It was like she was in a daze!

Amber then got up from the floor and just stared at me. Then she began to kick and hit at me.

Being that my hands were still tied up I couldn't fight with them. I tried to kick back at her with my tied together feet to defend myself. I couldn't fight back! With the way that Amber had me tied, I couldn't get my legs and feet to go where I wanted or needed them to go.

I saw Amber as she reached into her pocket and brought out the nail file she had teased me with earlier. She stabbed at me and I felt it pierce my arm. She waved it toward my face.

I couldn't shield myself. She dragged it across my left cheek down to my chin. I felt the blood coming from it. I knew I was going to bleed to death!

Amber then knocked me up against the wall in the closet and then she kicked me in the stomach. Again, I tried to bring my legs up to shield my body from the kicks! It wasn't doing much good! Amber stopped suddenly and just starred at me with those devilish green eyes.

All I could do was just hang from the chains. My body was sloped down against the wall and hanging toward the floor of the closet. My hands were tied together. My feet were bound together. I felt like a dangling puppet on a string. I was in horrific pain.

Then Amber said in her drunken voice, that her mother used to lock her in her room when she thought she had been a bad girl. She told me that her mother hated her! She said; just like you hate me, Sandy. Then she slammed the closet door shut.

Everything was quiet. It was dark. It seemed like hours had passed. As my eyes adjusted to the darkness, the only light that I could see was coming from under the door of the closet. The light was coming through from the bedroom window but it was fading away fast. I knew it must have been getting dark outside.

I knew that the electricity wouldn't be cut on until Monday and here I was all alone and eventually in total darkness.

As I rested from trying to fight back with Amber, I started thinking about everything Amber had said. I didn't hate Amber! I surely didn't understand her! Why was she comparing me to her mother?

As my thoughts swirled thru my mind, I managed to pull myself over and I leaned up closer against the wall of the closet. Thoughts kept going through my mind. Would Amber be back? Why was she doing this to me? How could I get out of this? Was I going to bleed to death?

All these thoughts and still I had no answers to my questions. At some point with all the thinking going on in my head and dealing with the pain I was in, I fell asleep or had passed out.

Later when I came to myself, I thought it was all a bad dream. Then I felt the ropes that tied my hands and feet. Then the chain rattled that had me bound in the closet. No it wasn't a dream! This was all too real!

I could see that a little bit of light was coming under the door. It must have been real early in the morning. It must have been Monday morning. My birthday gone! I was 40 years old! I again wondered where Amber was.

Feeling that I had strength, I kicked at the closed closet door. I wanted to bust it open! I yanked at the chains I was attached to. I wanted to pull them loose from the walls that they were attached to! I couldn't do anything. Exhausted, I just hung there.

Then I heard a phone ringing. It was my cell phone. I had recognized my ring tone. I figured Amber must have it! She must have taken it when she abducted me. Then it quit ringing!

About fifteen minutes later I heard someone coming up the stairs. Was it Amber? Was she going to beat on me again?

The stairs made creaking sounds as they were being stepped on. Then I heard as the footsteps had stopped just in front of the closet door. Then the closet door opened.

It was her! I saw that Amber had a paper plate in her hand. She set it down on my lap. It was four dry crackers on it. She had a small paper cup of water too. She set it on the floor of the closet just in front of me.

Amber reached and removed the tape from my mouth. She said now you eat these. This is all you'll get until supper. Then she said she had to go to work. She said she would be back shortly after the salon closes.

I could tell that Amber was sober now. I told her, begged her, to untie my hands so that I could eat the crackers she had brought. I hoped that I could trick her into letting me loose. If she untied my hands I would shove her away and get the heck out of there!

She said you know I can't do that, but I will leave your mouth uncovered so that you can eat. She said this place is so far away from anyone, that if you hollered, nobody would hear you.

She was right. Nobody ever traveled my road. It was strange but it was almost as if the good Amber was trying to return or so I thought!

Amber then bent down to me and hand fed the crackers to me. She held the water for me to drink. She took the paper plate and cup and tossed them into a nearby trash can.

She then stood up facing me and said in such a calm voice; I'm going to work now. Just as she started to turn to leave, she turned back to face me again. I didn't know what to expect of her.

Just before Amber had slammed the closet door shut, she kicked me in my side. I began screaming at her! Let me out! Don't leave me in here like this! I pleaded to her that I needed to go to the restroom! I heard Amber say through the closed door, if you can't hold it, then that's your problem. I then heard Amber going down the stairs. I heard a door close. Amber had left the house.

CHAPTER 15

SEVERE TORTURE

It was quiet. The time seemed to go by slowly. I had no way of knowing what time it was. I guessed it to be about 9am or later.

As I hung from the chains inside the closet, I thought about the fact that the electricity would be cut on today. Amber must have forgotten. She had left the tape off my mouth. I had a plan. I would listen for the power company to arrive. I would scream. The power man would rescue me. This would be God's way of getting me out of this! I waited!

I waited some more! That's all I could do. All the while, I still continued to kick at the closet door in hopes that it would open. I yanked at the chains that imprisoned me inside the closet until I was exhausted! No luck!

Time passes. It must have been lunch time. I was really getting hungry. I needed to go pee. Lord, I'd been holding it seems like forever! The cup of water for breakfast was wanting out. Thinking about it, I had held my bladder ever since Saturday night! Nearly two days!

What was I going to do? I didn't want to pee on myself! If I'd just quit thinking about it, maybe I could hold it longer! I had even tried to reposition myself to help hold my bladder! It was no use. I finally had to relieve myself. There was no stopping it! It was an awful feeling but it couldn't be helped. I had never felt so humiliated.

More time passes. I thought to myself, where is the power company? Surely they would be here today? Surely they didn't reschedule?

Then I thought I'd heard a vehicle. I listened! It was! I was screaming as loud as I could for someone to help me! Help me! I'm locked in a closet! Please help me!

I didn't think anyone heard me. Then I heard someone coming in. I could hear them coming up the stairs. They were running up the stairs! I hoped it wasn't Amber! I had to take my chance. I was screaming help me again!

The door knob to the closet was being turned and the door was opening. Someone had finally found me I thought! The power company had come!

The closet door flung open. It wasn't the power people but I saw that it was Todd. It was Amber's boyfriend.

I started telling him about what Amber had done to me. I was asking him to help me get loose and out of the closet!

He just shook his head no. He then started looking around the room. I saw him pick up the roll of tape that Amber had used on my mouth to keep me quiet.

He turned back to the closet! He quickly put the tape over my mouth to shut me up. All he had said was that Amber had forgotten that the electricity was to be turned on today. Then he said now we wouldn't want to spoil all the fun.

I knew then that Amber had gotten Todd to come and gag me! Todd left the room and then I heard him leave the house. I heard his vehicle drive away.

I began thinking about Todd knowing what was going on! What were he and Amber going to do to me? Was he behind this?

I was scared to death! What did they want from me? It couldn't be money! I didn't have any money! I knew in my heart that no matter what they wanted, they would kill me!

Sometime later I heard a vehicle again. Was it Todd coming back or was it the electric people? I couldn't scream but still I tried to.

I had to get out of this closet. I had to get out of this house. I was kicking at the door again. I jerked at the chains! It was no use. The door just wasn't opening. The chains weren't breaking loose!

I then heard a vehicle driving off. As the hours went by I knew that the electric people had been there. I could see light from under the door and it wasn't dimming as it had the day before. The power was on, and nobody knew I was there, except Amber and Todd.

I was so hungry. I tried not to think about food. I was thirsty too. A glass of iced tea would be real good now. That wouldn't do my bladder any good though! I tried not to think of anything but my mind wouldn't rest. I just wanted out of the dark closet.

I was mad. I tried to kick the door open once again. Nope! It wasn't opening! Hours passed.

The sound of a vehicle was nearing. I waited quietly. I recognized this vehicle. It was Amber's car. I had heard it so many times.

It must have been about 7:00pm. She must have just come from work. I was scared to move.

I heard her coming in the front door of the house and then I heard her foot steps as she walked up the stairs. I heard her keys rattling. She was coming into the bedroom.

She opened the closet door. She glared at me and said with hatred, I'll have your supper ready for you in a little while. Then she said you're beginning to smell bad. She was so cruel sounding.

Amber didn't come alone. I heard someone talking in another part of the house just outside the room I was being held captive in. It was Todd. I knew his voice! It sounded like he was on a phone with someone.

I tried to scream but it did no good. Still gagged, no sound came from my mouth. Nothing came out that was loud enough for any one to hear me. I had hoped that maybe whoever Todd was talking to would hear me if I could have screamed out! It was hopeless.

Amber left the room. She had left the closet door open. At least I could breathe now. I could see.

With my hands still tied and stretched up by the chains, I moved my arms toward my face. I brushed my arm across my face where Amber had cut me with the file.

I could tell that the blood had dried. I hoped that I hadn't lost a lot of blood. Maybe it wasn't as bad as I was thinking.

It wasn't but just a few minutes that Amber came back into the room. She had my so called supper in her hands. A cup of water and 4 crackers!

She said, now you be a good girl and eat your supper. I looked at the plate Amber had in her hand with the 4 crackers.

I tried to say to Amber, with a muffled voice, how do you expect one to survive with this little bit of what you call supper?

She must have understood me because she made the remark, well, I did!! I was so confused! What did Amber mean by saying she did?

Then she said if you think you can behave yourself, I will let you get cleaned up after supper.

I was thinking to myself, what had I done that Amber thought I needed to behave? I'd been tied up in a closet for God sakes. What was she talking about?

Amber removed the gag from my mouth. I was starving! I gobbled down the crackers and water as fast as Amber could feed them to me.

I was begging her to untie my hands. She wasn't listening! I begged to Amber to tell me why she was doing this to me. All along I was still trying to pull myself free. Amber would just mock everything I was saying, but she wouldn't answer me.

I then thought about the incident at the salon with the crackers. I started questioning Amber about that day. I began asking her about the time she said she hated crackers. I ask her about the time when she said she was full and had only eaten a few peanuts and sip of her drink!

She still didn't answer. She would say things like Polly want a cracker, or crackers for the hungry, over and over.

Then a while later Todd came to the bedroom door entrance and said to Amber, I have everything ready. Then he came over to the closet and stood next to Amber. They unchained me from the closet and untied my feet but kept my hands tied.

I was trying my best to get away, but Todd was so strong. Todd was holding me with one of his arms around my waist and the other around my throat!

Now I was standing in the middle of the bedroom floor as they undressed me! They were yanking my clothes from my body. The garments were coming apart at the seams as they ripped them off me!

Then Todd was leading me to the bath room. I saw Amber go into another room. It was then that I noticed Todd had on some sort of rubber like suit covering his entire body and hands. Then Amber reappeared. She also had on a rubber like suit totally covering her entire body and hands! I thought that was strange!

They had got me into the bathroom. Amber was holding me to keep me from getting away. I was trying so hard to escape.

Todd then wrapped a chain snuggly around my waist. He attached it to the shower bars above the tub. He untied my hands from the ropes and then retied one hand to the chain. WOW! I had one hand free! Apparently, Todd had gotten the bath water ready. I knew that it was hot because I could see the steam drifting up from the tub.

They made me step over into the tub of water. It was scalding hot! I was trying to refuse the bath, so Todd just pushed me down into the tub.

I found out very quick that it wasn't just water in the bathtub. It was like an acid! That explained the rubber suits that Todd and Amber were wearing. They didn't want to get burned!

The scalding hot acidy water was burning my skin like an icy fire. I was trying to get out of it. They wouldn't let me out. They said I had to wash myself before I could get out.

Amber was screaming at me the whole time. I couldn't believe some of the words that were coming from her mouth! She was saying you had better wash your self bitch! Whore! Slut! Those were the nice words!

Todd kept saying, Sandy, just do as Amber tells you to do! Stop fighting her! I was crying and begging them to let me out of the acid water. I begged them to stop what they were doing to me!

Begging didn't do me any good. I was trying to do as Amber wanted but the whole time I was still trying to get out. Todd kept pushing me back down into the burning water.

I guess I wasn't doing everything like Amber wanted me to do. Amber grabbed me by the hair. She poured shampoo over my head. She then started washing my hair. She then poured the acid like water over my head to rinse out the shampoo. It was burning me. It was running down my face and into my eyes.

My head was burning from where I'd been hit during this abduction. I figured it must have broken the skin. The acid like water was burning my face where Amber had cut me with the nail file.

Amber didn't care if she was hurting me. The more I cried, the rougher she would get with me.

I thought to myself, if I could just pull loose from this bar attaching me to the walls, I could get away. I would run! I would fight! I tried to break free. I yanked and pulled at the chain desperate to get loose! It was no use. The bar and chain was secure to the walls.

Now Todd had left the bathroom. I knew he was somewhere in the house so if I could have gotten away from Amber, he would probably catch me!

Horror came! I saw Amber reach for an electric razor. It was on a shelf that we had put up when fixing the house up.

She plugged the razor into the electrical outlet on the wall. She turned it on. She was dangling it over the tub of water with me still in it.

Though horrified, I screamed at her. Go ahead and drop it! You've already hurt me bad enough! At this point I didn't care if I lived or died. I screamed to Amber about the fact that at least I knew if I died, I'd be with God!

Amber acted like what I had said to her had made her mad. She said, I'm not done with you yet and as for your God, I hope that he helps you more than he ever helped me. She was now screaming at me. She screamed that when she had called to him as a child he was never there for her. She said "as far as I'm concerned, there is not a God.

Amber then slung the electric razor against the wall. It shattered all over the bathroom floor and out into the door way.

She called to Todd to come and help her get me out of the tub. I sure wasn't fighting to stay in that tub! I was thanking God that they were finally letting me get out. Todd did as Amber had asked him then went out again.

By this time I was too weak to fight back. Amber led me back to the bedroom where she had kept me before.

I was still naked. I felt so helpless. I begged her; please don't put me back into that closet. Not because I begged, but she said I'm not going to put you back in there. We need to get you prettied up.

I had no idea of what she was going to do next! She called to Todd again. He came into the room. He and Amber tied me in a chair. Then she had Todd to bring her work bag to her. He did as she asks.

I knew by now that all this had to be of Amber's doings and Todd had just got caught up in it all.

I watched as Amber opened her work bag and laid out all of her manicure tools and hair styling things on a dresser.

She reached inside the bag again. She pulled out a bottle of whiskey. She turned it up to her mouth and drank almost half of the bottle before she put it down. She set the half empty bottle on the dresser.

She then had Todd help her pull the chair I was tied in, up to the mirror that was over the dresser. By this time my hands were strapped with ropes to the chair arms. There was no way I was going any where but I was not giving up trying!

Amber said to me, let's play beauty shop! Amber then picked up a hair dryer and plugged it into the outlet.

I was trying to get free from the chair! I couldn't break the ropes! The ropes were hurting and burning my arms as I pulled them!

She held the hair dryer up to my head with the heat set to high. She was not trying to dry my hair. She was burning my scalp. She wouldn't stop.

I begged and pleaded with her to please stop! My head felt like it was on fire! I could smell my hair and scalp burning!

It seemed like she would never stop! Then she put the dryer aside. She then grabbed up a curling iron that she had plugged into the wall outlet. She touched her finger to it, then shouted, owe, that's hot!!

She brought the hot iron toward me. She laid the iron to my neck and face. She rolled the iron over my arms and other parts of my body. I smelled my flesh burning. I could feel and see the skin rolling up as I was being burned all over my body! I was screaming!

Not quick enough for me, she finally put down the curling iron. I was terrified of what she might do next. Amber was pretty liquored up now. The whiskey was working on her.

I saw Amber take out a pair of scissors. She started cutting my hair. She took my hair by the handfuls and was pulling it. She didn't care if the scissors was stabbing my head. The scissors was cutting what hair she didn't pull out by hand or what had fallen out from being burned from the hair drier.

I could see what Amber was doing to me in the mirror. I tried not to look, but Amber would grab my face and make me look. She said if I didn't watch her I'd never learn to be a good beautician.

Amber then took out her nail file. She grabbed my right hand and started to file on my nails. Once again, the ropes that were holding my hands to the arms of the chair were burning as she jerked my hands around.

She then started filing on the nails of my left hand. She filed on my nails of both hands until they were bleeding. The fingernails of both hands had been filed beyond the skin. Whenever I tried to resist from what she was doing to me, she would stab me in the arms, legs, or anywhere she could with the file. Even though I was exhausted I was still trying to fight back.

Amber didn't like me fighting her one little bit. She would say to me in her drunken voice, sit still and quit moving and let me do this. She said I was making things worse on myself!

What would she expect someone to do? Just laugh about all this! I was begging to Amber to tell me why she was doing this to me? She wouldn't answer me.

Amber then took out a cuticle stick and began to push the cuticles on my fingers so far back that the skin tore from the nails. I knew that I would lose my nails! I was screaming. I was crying. I was bleeding. I was begging her to stop.

Next Amber picked up a pair of eye tweezers and started plucking out all of my eyebrows. She pulled them out one brow at a time. My eyes were red and swollen by the time she had finished! My face was beginning to look like it wasn't a face.

The strange thing that kept happening was that every now and then I'd see Todd stick his head in around the door. I wondered if he was worried about me.

Maybe he couldn't stand to watch Amber do these terrible things to me! If so, why didn't he try to stop Amber's torture on me? Then I thought maybe he was just keeping a look out for Amber? I guessed he was concerned about her.

I wondered if he and Amber were thinking that someone might come looking for me? I was praying that someone would come around and find me!

As if what Amber had done to me already wasn't enough, I saw Amber reach for a bottle of rubbing alcohol! I began screaming as Amber poured the rubbing alcohol into my hands and over my nails. I thought I was going to die. It burned like fire!

I wondered if this was Amber's way of thinking that she was sterilizing the wounds. Then she dashed alcohol into my face! I clinched my eyes shut just in time, even though I still felt the stinging from it! I just kept trying to keep my eyes closed as the alcohol was dripping down from the corners of my eyes.

I couldn't believe what was happening to me! I was still screaming, crying and trying to break free from all of this torture!

CHAPTER 16

CLOSE CALLS

As the torture continued, I heard a phone ring. I believed it was my cell phone! I recognized the ring tone!

Amber quickly stopped her torture on me! Then she ran out of the room staggering. She then came back with the phone which was still ringing. It was my cell phone!

She said, drunkenly, that I had been a popular girl today. She said everybody had tried to call me, but all they had gotten was a voice mail message.

She stated to me that lucky "her" that I had made the remark to everyone that I was turning off my cell phone! That was going to make things easier, she had said!

The phone then quit ringing. Amber began to tell me that I had some messages waiting and said that I needed to check them. She wanted me to punch in my code to open the mail box. She insisted that I give her the code so that she'd be able to check and clear any future messages that I might get later.

When I refused to do so, she started slapping me in the face and on my head with one hand and stabbing me with the nail file with the other.

She was screaming at me. She didn't want anyone to get suspicious she had said. She threatened to kill me!

I was scared that Amber was going to kill me! It was hard to do with my fingers still bleeding, but I managed to do as she said. I punched my code number 82407 as I verbally spoke them to Amber. Blood was getting all over my cell phone as I punched in the numbers. Amber wrote down the numbers on a note pad that was lying on the dresser.

As the messages began to play, Amber had put the phone on speaker so I could here them. One message was from Tammy. It said Hi, its Tammy; guess you did turn your phone off. Hope you are having a great time in Vegas. I can't wait to see you when you get home. Everything here is fine. Love ya.

Another was from Pam. She just said Hi, its Pam. Hope your hitting the jack pot at the casinos. See ya soon. We all miss you. Bye!

There was another message and then another. The voice mail was full. After all the messages had played, Amber cleared them and she tucked the phone away into her pocket.

I prayed that somehow, someone would realize something wasn't right. Then I thought of Jerry. I knew that he would call me soon. He had always called between his gigs! I knew that he had another gig to do down in Texas. He would be there by now!

Before he had left, he had told me that he would call me as soon as he had gotten into a room. He would call me with his room number.

If I didn't answer the phone when he called for me he would know that something was wrong. He knew that I always answered my phone when he called but if I didn't answer at that instant, he knew I'd call him back ASAP. Jerry would get me help! At least I wanted to believe that he would! I needed something to hang on for!

My thoughts were distracted when I heard Amber call Todd into the room. She was making him gather some clothes from out of a bag that she had placed over in a corner of the room.

Amber and Todd started putting the clothes on me. Todd was doing most of the dressing of me. He was gazing and touching my body. I hated him for that!

Amber must have not seen that Todd was touching me. She would have exploded. She was a very jealous person.

I knew that Amber was really zapped from the liquor. She didn't seem to hear me when I would tell Todd to stop touching me!

Finally, not soon enough for me, my body was dressed. I was in such awful pain that even the clothes being placed on my body hurt me.

Todd and Amber tied and chained me back into the dark closet. Todd put the gag back over my mouth. Amber then slammed the closet door to shut it.

By this time Todd had to hold Amber up, as she was so drunk that she barely could hold onto the door when she had slammed it closed.

Even though Amber was dog drunk, Todd was still doing as Amber told him to do. I heard her tell Todd to get her out of there! He did as she said! Todd had closed the bedroom door behind them when they had exited. I had heard it slam shut.

Suddenly it was quiet. What were Amber and Todd doing? Where had they gone? The time seemed to creep by. I listened for a while. It seemed the house was empty. Amber and Todd had gone.

Sleep! I didn't sleep! I was afraid to close my eyes! I was in fear for my life! I was afraid that Amber and Todd would return to kill me. I was so hungry! I was cold! I was scared! I was hurting!

CHAPTER 17

THE RAPE

It was Tuesday morning. I couldn't focus on much. I guess I had lost a lot of blood from my fingers and body. I was weak! I felt dehydrated! I was shivering!

Maybe someone would find me if I could just hang on until Wednesday. That was if Amber and Todd didn't kill me first! Everyone would be expecting me back from the trip to Vegas that I was supposedly to have gone on. Surely someone would realize I was missing and come find me!

Why hadn't Jerry found me yet? I wondered had he tried to call? Was he aware that something was wrong? Didn't he wonder why I hadn't called him? Was I going to die? I worried if Amber and Todd might have done something to hurt Jerry? Would I ever see him or my friends again?

I knew it was late in the morning. Where were Amber and Todd? Had Amber gone to work? I was so hungry! I didn't want them to come back but I needed food. I was going to die of starvation.

My thoughts were interrupted when I heard a noise. It was someone. I prayed that it would be someone that would help me. I heard the creaking of the stairs as someone was getting closer to the bedroom.

Even though I felt weak, I was trying to kick the door and was pulling at the chains holding me in the closet. The chain snapped loose.

I was trying to get to the door knob of the closet door. My hands were still tied with ropes and they were in so much pain. My hands were on the door knob! I was trying to turn it! I wasn't sure how, but somehow the door swung open!

I was trying to crawl out from the closet! It was hard to crawl with my feet and legs still tied together but I wasn't giving up!

Then I saw the shoes of someone. I looked up! It was Todd. He quickly jerked me up and flung me back into the closet. He pulled the tape from my mouth.

I begged and pleaded to Todd to let me go. He said he couldn't do that. He said Amber wouldn't like that much. He said Amber would never forgive him or marry him if he released me.

He then started undoing the ropes from my feet and legs. I wondered why he would untie me after saying Amber wouldn't like it.

Then all of a sudden he started ripping my blouse open. Oh my God, he was going to rape me!

I was trying to fight back! I was begging him to stop! I felt him tug at my under garment. He succeeded to remove them. He was pushing my skirt up and then I felt him enter inside me as he roughly pressed himself to my body.

I continued to try and fight him off! I wasn't having any luck with it! My hands were still tied and the pain of my fingers was unbearable when I tried to push him off me.

Again I begged him to stop. I screamed at him and told him he was hurting me. He was so strong. He wouldn't stop!

Finally it was over. Todd got off of me. He then retied me and chained me back into the closet. Then he said, as if nothing had even happened, that Amber would be back here after she got off from work.

He said if I told Amber about what had happened I'd be dead for sure! Todd closed the closet door. I was screaming and praying and asking God why was all of this happening to me?

I knew that Todd was still in the bedroom. I could hear him shuffling around outside the closet door. I wondered what he was doing.

A few minutes passed. The closet door was being opened again. That's when I saw Todd with a plate of 4 crackers and a cup of water in his hand.

He reached down to me and shoved the crackers into my mouth. He poured the water into my mouth but most of it was going in the floor.

He then put tape back over my mouth to keep me quiet! When finished, he slammed the door shut again!

I heard the creaking of the stairs. I heard a door slam shut. I heard a vehicle drive away. Thank God Todd had left!

I felt so dirty. What was going to happen to me next? I began to pray! GOD WHERE ARE YOU? PLEASE GOD, DON'T LET ME DIE?

As I was praying I began to cry. I cried myself to sleep wondering if God had heard any of my prayers.

CHAPTER 18

AMBER PULLS THE TRIGGER

I awoke. I wasn't sure what time it was, but I thought it had to be Tuesday night. A noise from inside the house had awakened me. Amber must have been home from work I thought.

I could hear someone coming up the stairs. Then I heard someone in the hallway of the house upstairs. They hadn't come into the room where I was locked up!

What if it wasn't Amber? Who was there? I couldn't scream because Todd had gagged my mouth when he had left me earlier. What good would it do anyway?

Then I heard Amber and Todd talking. It was both of them! They had come back. I was terrified!

I couldn't make out everything they were saying but I did here Amber say something about a call from my cell phone. I heard her say something about Amelia. There voices were fading.

Then I heard them running and bumping around. It seemed that they were going back down the stairs. Then it got quiet. I heard a door close. Maybe they were leaving? I heard another door slam. Everything was quiet again.

Then suddenly I heard someone coming up the stairs again! I could hear the creaking stairs as they were running. Someone was coming back!

Suddenly the closet door flung open. It was Amber. She stood facing me. Her eyes seemed to be looking right through me. She had a gun in her hand! She was pointing it right straight to my head!

She said your friend Amelia has left you a message. Amber said by the time Amelia gets to you, it will be too late.

Amber began telling me that Amelia had called the Las Vegas hotel where I was supposed to have been staying. The hotel clerk had told Amelia that I had never arrived.

Amber said to me that Amelia's message says she was coming to your house and if you got the message to call her.

Amber said, Lucky for her, they wouldn't find me at home! Then Amber said and they are so stupid that they wouldn't ever think of looking for me at the old cabin home. I figured Amber was probably right. They wouldn't think of this place! What was I going to do!

Amber jerked the gag from my mouth. I was still hanging from the chains attaching me into the closet! I was trying to pull free! I was pulling with everything I had left in me! The chains had me bound! I wasn't going anywhere!

I started screaming at Amber! I begged her to not shoot me. Just leave. I won't tell anyone about this.

I was even screaming for Todd to come and help me even though he had raped me! I wasn't even sure if he was still anywhere around. I was desperate.

I was again yanking at the chains in hopes that they'd pull loose from the closet walls! It wasn't happening! The chains were snuggly intact!

I kept asking Amber why? Why have you done this to me? What have I done to you to deserve this? I don't understand, I told her!

Amber then said, with hatred, that her mother hated her when she was a child. Her mother had always left her by herself. Her mother would lock her in her room for days at a time and the only thing her mother ever fed her was crackers and water each day while being locked up. That's why I hate crackers, she said!

Then Amber stated to me that her mother had treated her just like I had treated her. She told me that now her mother is gone! Dead! Just like I was going to be gone! She said how does it feel Sandy?

My mind began to think of so many thoughts. Oh my God! Did Amber think of me as her mother? Did Amber shoot and kill her mother? Had she been abused as a child? What had happened to Amber?

I watched as Amber threw my cell phone down onto the floor of the closet. My attention was brought back to the gun!

The look I saw in Amber's eyes, I knew what was next! I screamed NO AMBER! She raised the gun toward me! The gun went off and I felt the bullet from the gun as it hit me in the head. My body went limp.

Though blood was running down into my eyes, I could see Amber leaving the room. She was leaving me to die.

I heard her running down the stairs. I heard a door slam! I could here a car leaving. Tires were squealing.

I then thought about my cell phone. I could barely see it lying on the closet floor through the blood that was dripping down into my eyes and face. I tried to reach for it. I realized that I couldn't feel my hands!

I thought I had felt something with my toes of one foot. I thought it was the cell phone. I hoped it was! The other foot didn't seem to have any feeling to it!

I realized that my toe was touching my cell phone! I tried to use my toes to punch in numbers on the phone. I didn't know what numbers I was pushing or for that matter if any! For all I knew I could have been hitting the off button.

Then finally, I could hear that the phone was ringing someone. I started praying that someone would answer. It rung many times! I was giving up.

Then I heard a voice. I couldn't speak. I tried but nothing came from my mouth. The faint voice I had heard coming thru the phone was saying it's going to be alright. I'm coming. I'm coming!

CHAPTER 19

THE RESCUE

As I dangled lifeless like inside the closet, I felt myself going in and out of consciousness. I just knew I was going to die!

I wasn't sure of how much time had passed, but it seemed like a lifetime, when I heard sirens and they were nearing.

Then I heard someone trying to get into the house. Someone was seriously trying to break the door down. I tried to scream! Again, no sound came from my mouth.

Then I heard voices speaking and I heard feet running through the house and then up the stairs. I thought praise God, someone has come!

What was taking them so long to get to me! In my mind everything seemed to be going in slow motion.

Finally, I heard someone say "she's in here"! I found her! I was trying to lift my eyes toward the door. I could barely see with all of the blood still running into my eyes as my body hung from the chains that held me into the closet.

I saw an image of someone. I thought it was Amelia. She was my dearest best friend in the whole world. Jerry was with her. The image I saw was confirmed when I heard

Amelia saying to someone that she had picked Jerry up from the airport and that they had rushed here to find me.

I could see that there were paramedics and cops everywhere. I could hear Amelia telling someone that Jerry and she new something was wrong when I hadn't return their phone calls. I heard them say that's when they had called the police.

They were saying that they had gone to my house and no one was at home. They then said they thought about the old cabin house! They had then guided the police to the house that we had fixed up for Amber! They didn't know it, but they had hopefully saved my life.

I felt something or someone touch my face. It was Jerry. He was asking me who had done this to me!

I tried to speak. My mouth was moving, but no sound was coming out from it! Jerry couldn't hear me he had said! He couldn't understand me!

I kept trying to tell Jerry, Amelia and the cops what had happen and who had done this to me. They still didn't understand.

Jerry finally mentioned Amber's name. He was asking me where Amber was. I, with all the strength I could muster, began to rock my head from side to side! I tried to blink my eyes! They knew from my reaction, or at least I hoped they knew, that it was Amber that had done this to me.

The next thing I knew was that I was being lifted into an ambulance. I could hear the siren's blasting. I knew that it was pouring rain outside as the droplets of rain had hit upon my face when I was put into the ambulance. Then the sound of the thunder was drowning out the loud sirens as the thunder roared! The lightning was so vivid and bright as it lit up the dark skies!

Though I couldn't see, I tried to watch as the paramedics were working on me. They were trying to keep me alive. I could hear them saying "stay with us Sandy"! Hang on girl!

I must say beware!!! Amber and Todd are still out there! Somewhere!!!

Be watching for: Days of Torture "Return of Amber"